W9-CTH-024

FEB 19 2023

Magnolia Library

PRAISE FOR APRIL FOOL'S DAY

"An ambitious first novel ... The magic realism of the final sections is exemplary; Novakovich has found his groove." —*Washington Post*

"[Ivan] is a fully rounded character, the type of protagonist...that we rarely find in fiction." —*Chicago Tribune*

"Delightfully neurotic . . . Novakovich brings a deft touch to his ambitious and unconventional first novel." —*Columbus Dispatch*

"APRIL FOOL'S DAY is a wonder...[It] has an economy of style and narrative that all good readers will relish." —*Republic of Letters*

"A heartfelt novel about the war-torn Balkans that's actually quite funny... and touching." —*GQ*

"Both humorous and horrifying as it traces one man's misadventures." — *USA Today*

"Wickedly funny and deeply harrowing...Novakovich knows how to tell a story...Strange, lyrical beauty abounds here." —*New York Times Book Review*

"Disturbing and frequently beautiful...the novel is a Balkan conflation of Louis-Ferdinand Celine, Gogol's DEAD SOULS, and SLAUGHERHOUSE FIVE." —*Minneapolis Star Tribune*

"[A] laugh-while-you-grimace novel...[Novakovich] writes with dark wit, and a touching sympathy." —*Newsweek International*

NO LONGER PROPERTY OF
SEATTLE PUBLIC LIBRARY

"Rife with dark humor [and] notable for its witty reflections on politics, literature and the vicissitudes of the human heart." —*San Diego Union-Tribune*

RUBBLE
OF
RUBLES

—A NOVEL—

JOSIP NOVAKOVICH

DZANC
BOOKS

2580 Craig Rd.
Ann Arbor, MI 48103
www.dzancbooks.org

RUBBLE OF RUBLES Copyright © 2022, text by Josip Novakovich. All rights reserved, except for brief quotations in critical articles or reviews. No part of this
book may be reproduced in any manner without prior written permission from
the publisher: Dzanc Books, 2580 Craig Rd., Ann Arbor, MI 48103.

Library of Congress Catalog-in-Publication Data available upon request.

ISBN: 9781950539642
First US edition: December 2022
Cover design by Steven Seighman
Interior design by Michelle Dotter

Printed in the United States of America

10   9   8   7   6   5   4   3   2   1

For my big kids, Eva and Joseph

CHAPTER ONE

A quick ride through Sankt Peterburg

ON BOLSHOI PROSPEKT on Vasilievski Ostrov, I raised my hand to hail down a cab, and a black BMW stopped. It was magic—you raise a finger, and voila, a fancy car pulls up. This was before Uber when any driver could stop and give you a lift.

A middle-aged man with short, silvery hair and a broken nose lowered the window. I offered two hundred rubles. The man asked for three hundred.

—But it's not far, only to Kresty Prison on Arsenalskaya.

—In this traffic, it could take a while. *Vyi anglichanin*? How much would it cost in London?

—We are not in London.

—Fifteen pounds, which is seven hundred rubbles.

—Two-fifty.

—*Suda*! said the man and pointed to the front seat.

—I want to sit in the back.

—You sit in front. I am not your servant. This is not Deutschland. We will be colleagues during the ride. And you talk so I don't fall asleep.

I sat on the cold black leather of the front seat.

The cabby—although of course, like most people in Russia who offered rides in the streets, he was not a cabby—drove quickly over the Palace Bridge and down Nevsky. I pulled the seatbelt to click it.

—*Ne nada*, said the driver. —I am very good driver; you are safer in the car than out there.

—It's still a good idea to put on a seatbelt.

—That's for cowards.

—I don't want to be brave; I am just taking a ride!

—You are safe.

—But isn't it the law to wear seatbelts?

—Da, on paper. We don't bother with such trivial things. Perhaps in a few years it will be a real law after enough of us die on the roads.

—I think enough people have died on the roads in Russia.

—Not nearly enough.

My driver was checking out something on his Blackberry, and without looking at the road, he accelerated. Two policemen in blue-gray with their billy clubs waved us down in front of the pink old Duma. The driver jumped out of the car. He was back in a minute.

—That was *ochen bistro*, I said. How did you manage to get off? Was it expensive?

—I showed them my badge. I am a police officer, ranked major. They are nothing, dirt of the road. They backed off and apologized.

—An officer? But you have no uniform. And you have no respect for the laws.

—High-ranking officers don't wear uniforms. I have one for parades and presidential visits, in the trunk. And the laws are for the commoners.

—Why did they have to apologize? You were obviously speeding.

—Yes, doing you a favor, my friend, so you can get to where you are going as fast as possible.

—I am not in such a terrible rush.

—When was there an American who was not rushing in Russia?

—I want to relax from the rat race.

—We have lots of rats. I bet our rats are tougher than yours.

—Rat race is a metaphor.

—I've watched *Law and Order*. You Americans love that expression, and you love rats. For relaxation, I would recommend Lake Baykal. My aunt owns a house, she wouldn't charge you much. How much could you pay? One thousand dollars a month, fair price?

—No, thank you, I like it here.

—Beautiful? Yes?

—Yes.

—It's ugly. As soon as I have enough money for gas, I am going out to my dacha. You are my dacha gas.

—Thank you. I've never been called anything more flattering than that, dacha gas.

—You want to visit Kresty?

—Yes, of course.

—It's an ugly old prison. What's there to see?

—I don't know. I read about it—amazing history.

—And how do you want to visit?

—What do you mean, how?

—As a tourist or in some other capacity?

—Of course, tourist. What other option is there? Prisoner?

The driver laughed, his body shaking, and ended with a snort. — Not a journalist? You are not going to write bad things about Russia?

—No, not a journalist. There's nothing bad to say about Russia. Other than that journalists get shot here. It's a beautiful country.

—It's a horrible country, full of crooks and thieves. I know. It's my job to know.

His Blackberry rang out the Nuremberg rally speech—many Russians delight in choosing unusual ringtones—and he answered and talked fast and listened and talked, and parked on the side of the road, outside of Borye Gallery and Café, and waited. On the other side of the road was the somber Bolshoi Dom, the old KGB head-quarters. A stately brunette in a fur coat talked on her cellphone and looked in our direction.

—I thought we were in a rush! I said.

—I'm waiting for a call.

Soon the phone howled again, but the driver didn't answer it. He drove off, scorching the pavement. At a crossing before the Litenyi Bridge, he ran a red light and drove close to the curb where a pedestrian was standing. Two men pushed the pedestrian, who flew out onto the road.

The driver swerved toward the curb and smashed the pedestrian. I jerked up to the dashboard but avoided hitting it.

—Damned pedestrians, they are so aggressive in this town! He shouldn't have been standing on the curb. He jumped right in front of me, to wave me down, did you see that? He has no right to do that.

—Somebody pushed him.

—He was staggering drunk, tripped over a cobble or something.

—And you swerved to hit him! You didn't have to go so close to the curb, look how wide the street is.

He glared at me, his thick black eyebrows arched. I lowered my gaze and concentrated on the driver's nose. The hairs sticking from his nostril were sparse yet bunched together pointedly like the remnants of an overused aquarelle detail paintbrush.

—You want to write about this for a newspaper?

—I am not going to write about it, but why did you swerve? And I am sure nobody would be interested in a . . .

—Oh yes, people would be interested.

—How do you know?

—I didn't swerve. You may have drunk a little too much and straight lines look crooked to you.

—Aren't you going to stop to call the ambulance?

—Someone will pick him up. I will see to that.

—Should we call the police?

—I am the police.

—But this is an emergency.

—First I'll get you to your destination.

—You don't have to. I am not in a rush. Can you call an ambulance?

—What's the hurry?

—He's lying in the street, dying.

The BMW accelerated over the Litenyi drawbridge, which sloped gently over the Niva. The tires hummed over the stretches of grates and bumped over the drawbridge elbows. Ahead on the left gleamed the pointed golden tower of the Peter and Paul fortress, and many sunbathers, mostly men, stood, visible from the distance like a defrocked toy army. That was the fashion here, for men to be standing while sunbathing; with the low-angled sun, you get more sunshine that way. And moreover, you can look around and have a better perspective.

—He's bleeding in the street! I said.

—How would you know? You can see across the bridge?

—You may have killed him.

—Be calm. You Americans dramatize everything. You don't know Russian alcoholics. They are made of rubber; nothing can harm them. My car only brushed him.

—It was a head-on! You might want to examine your bumper and your right headlight. I bet your *mashina* is damaged.

—This thing is sturdy, like a tank. Made in Deutschland.

—I give up. I don't need the ride anymore.

—We aren't there yet. Wait a minute.

—We are close enough, I can walk. I want to walk.

—I am a man of my word. I promised to get you there and I insist. I can't stop on the bridge.

—But I want to walk.

—Fine. The driver turned onto the Arsenal Embankment and braked suddenly. There you go! Enjoy the prison. It's very impressive, worth spending some time! You could stay there for days, months, years.

I gave him three hundred rubles.

—Wait, I'll find fifty.

—I don't need the fifty.

—*Vsevo dobrova*, and if you get into trouble, you can call me. You want my number?

—Thank you. I don't get into trouble.

—You don't? What were you in now if not trouble? You think that was no trouble?

—Well, no trouble for me.

—This is Russia, my friend. Everybody in trouble. And nobody sees anything. And Kresty? Don't go there. You are better off going to the Mariinsky, see something beautiful. If you ever need a ride, give me a call, and I'll get you there, fast and reliable. I can always use a bit of dacha gas.

Should I call the police to check on the hit pedestrian? But wasn't I just with a policeman? He probably wasn't lying. But then, maybe he was lying all the way, and was no policeman, and had bribed the cops. Did he follow me?

I took a leisurely stroll toward Kresty. I suddenly had a yearning to go home, back to New York. What's the point of walking the streets of the insane country? Ah, the hell with it, I'll stay, and I am not responsible for what I see here. This would all be going on without me being here. Is it some kind of Heisenberg's principle of uncertainty, a Schrödinger's Cat, that we don't know how the atom behaves when it's not observed but only when it is observed, and that phenomenological subjectivity, if it applies to an atom, how much more should it apply to such a universe of molecules as St. Petersburg? How would I know if St. Petersburg would be the same without me? Without me, perhaps this man wouldn't have been hit on Litenyi. It's easy to think that I am the superfluous man, that everything would be the same without me, but how would I know that? Maybe everything is what it is because I am here and observing it, and my observing it is influencing its behavior, getting an element of extra frenzy out of it because my mind is frantic and paranoid. Paranoid? Strange things are happening.

What the hell was I doing in Russia? I had abandoned my banking career in New York, which ended after I'd put nearly all my clients' money (and mine) into vanishing Enron stocks, and after an eighty-year-old client of mine killed himself. He jumped off his Miami Beach penthouse legs first, burying his well-preserved leonine head in his own remains. It was a shock to me that my investing games neither resulted in delighting my clients nor in my amassing wealth. I could have gritted my teeth through the crisis and emerged triumphant and rich and helpful to many after a few mistakes, but I lost the taste for it and for that kind of American dream.

Now in the serious years when I should be making loads of money so I could retire (although I lost respect for retirement), my head absorbed the stories from Russia—*Brothers Karamazov* and tales of Leskov and Gogol. These gloomy tales elated me—I didn't have to read tedious stock market reports nor minutes from Berkshire meetings. During the times of Christ all the way to the times of Dante, thirty-three to thirty-five were the years of self-examination, the middle of life's journey, but with improved health care now it was around forty-eight. It should be nothing to fret about—in fact, midlife is a luxury if you imagine that you still have as much time left as you've already wasted. The very mid in midlife expresses hubris concerning one's prospects. Midlife didn't appear to me as anything negative, but an opportunity: a year of serious contemplation and insights. Most of my colleagues at Solomon Brothers planned to retire by the age of fifty, to write that novel that was lurking in them—yet another murder mystery? Wasn't a bank the beginning of it all, the quintessential American murder story, Bonnie & Clyde? It frightened me that even the apparently sane people delight in murder stories. You see dignified gentlemen and imagine they are thinking of the Chinese stock market, blowjobs, and yachts, but they are daydreaming of slaughter. When they walk aggressively in the street and grind their porcelain teeth, they may dream of pushing a knife into your breastbone.

CHAPTER TWO

Encountering the living and the dead

Two days later, still jetlagged, I walked out of the apartment I was renting on the Griboedova Embankment. The rusty elevator box overshot the ground floor by a foot. I stepped into a dank hallway. A cat's eyes fluoresced on the second step of the staircase. My nostrils constricted from the smell of urine as I tried to decipher if it was human or feline. After the iron door banged shut behind me, I walked out to the Embankment of Canal Griboedova, admiring the buildings' thick walls, which looked ancient, like a cross between well-preserved Roman ruins and ill-built fallout shelters, even though the city, at 303 years of age—this was in Anno Domini 2006—was relatively young.

My American cell phone didn't work here. At a used cell phone store at the Gostiny Dvor metro station, I bought an old-style Nokia. The shop assistant used his passport to register my SIM card.

—Why do you need to register the SIM card?

—So the police can monitor you. It's the law. Without registration, you can't use a cell phone in Russia.

—Couldn't they monitor me anyway?

—Just don't buy drugs using the phone, he said, and don't kill anybody. If you do, don't talk on the phone about it, or they might look for me.

—I like your joke.

—No joke. You never know what people will do, but you look harmless.

I didn't take that as a compliment. In Russia it's better to look dangerous. I noticed he had a black gun behind him, on a bookshelf among many Nokias.

—You have a gun, why?

—So people wouldn't steal cell phones from me. Just the other day, a couple of kids tried, but when I grabbed the gun, they ran away.

He lifted it and aimed it at my forehead and laughed, revealing his misaligned teeth.

Although seeing the gun like that was startling, I was still sleepy and photosensitive. The light reflecting off the windows of Dom Knygi made me squint. I entered Café Mocha, on Pushkinskaya, a grassy boulevard off Nevsky Prospect.

As I sat down, three young women dressed in white pranced out of the café. With their ponytails swinging, I had an equine association; the click-clack of the blue stiletto heels on the terracotta tiles sounded like hooves on cobblestones. The equestrian femmes fatales marched out with a determined air, as though on their way to whip France in a Davis Cup semifinal. Was one of them Dementieva? Russian names can give you strange associations, demented. And Putin? Well, the puns are obvious. I am not going to put them in here.

After me walked in a remarkably poised brunette with a pearl necklace over her tanned neck and breastbone and sat at a table next to mine. Then she got up and hung her fur coat on a hanger and sat back and lit a thin cigarette.

I'd heard that good coffee in Russia was hard to find and that it was ridiculously cheap. The coffee, however, was joltingly excellent and overpriced, six dollars for a double macchiato.

I picked up *St. Petersburg Times*, and after an article about the mad rise in real estate prices, there was a report about a Georgian wine exporter killed in a hit-and-run accident on Liteny, possibly an assassination. I gulped the double macchiato.

I looked over to the next round-top table at the brunette seated straight, her legs crossed, with thin ankles and delineated calves accented by deep and straight grooves. Maybe a former ballerina? Why not a current one? I found her presence electrifying. Should I talk to her? I felt insecure in Russian, although I'd minored in Russian in college, in search of Slavic roots. My father (English-Czech), while working as an economic advisor in Belgrade, married my Slovenian mother. (She had a famous uncle, writer Louis Adamic, who was shot at his home in New Jersey, probably assassinated by the Yugoslav secret police. Why would the secret police bother with writers?)

My neighbor was smiling minimally, enigmatically. Maybe there was a bit of a cynical sideways curl to her scarlet-glossed lips? She spread a book in front of her, *English Grammar,* and sighed.

—How is your English? I asked.

—Bad, that's why I learn. You American?

—How did you know?

—I knew right away your continent.

—By my jeans and sneakers?

—You stare at girls.

—I didn't stare.

—Russian men not interested. Only Americans and Italians do it. And you don't look Italian.

Her voice was deep and sandy like a smoking Italian actress's.

—I don't look Italian? I could be Dutch or German.

—They civilized.

—We are civilized! In fact, we have civilized the globe—rock and roll, the pill, Boeing, and Microsoft.

—Micro soft? Small and soft?

—Jumbo-jet, Boeing.

She lit up her ultra-thin brown cigarette. The paper and the tobacco were of the same hue, and the brown hue matched her brown eyes and the brown hair in a deep relaxing monochrome.

—I must go.

She left the burning cigarette leaning against the ashtray. The thin stick was red at both ends, from the lipstick and the steady smoldering.

—My name is David, and yours?

—They call me Masha.

—Who are they? I asked, and then realized that she'd simply translated the Russian *Menya zovut* . . .

—They? Masha said and looked around the room.

—How about meeting for coffee again? I said.

—Simple like that?

She focused on my face and squinted a little, her eyelashes unnaturally long and curvy.

—I can give you an English lesson in exchange for a Russian lesson.

She wrote her phone number on the napkin with her brown eyeliner, and then, on the way out, waved to me, but didn't smile. Her gaze lingered on my chest. Was my shirt dirty? Or did I have something in the shirt pocket? Thankfully, the bit of extra fat didn't translate into truck-driver-style boobs.

Her abandoned cigarette was spinning out a bluish trail of smoke. I stood and picked up the cigarette and snubbed it in the glass ashtray. I paid the bill, one red and one blue note, and then three large five-ruble coins for the tip, which rattled on the tip tray.

—*Eto vsyo*? Is that all? the cashier asked. More rubbles! You pay for your friend?

—She didn't pay?

—Gentlemen pay, a little Russian rule.

—Russian roulette?

—Four hundred rubbles.

—Rubbles? I think you'd prefer rubles.

I handed over four hundred and fifty rubles.

On the way home, I had a couple of bliny with red caviar at Coffee Break. Caviar was cheap and available even in dives over white bread and butter. Oval translucent eggs looked like albino eyes spooned out of little creatures. Maybe each egg was an eye, seeing into the future. They burst on my tongue, and I shivered as you usually do when something is tasty and slimy, appealing and repulsive, and this state between desire and disgust energized me. Caviar: it is life, was life, will be life.

At the corner of Griboedova and Lomonosova, I entered a diesel cloud containing a human body spread limply in front of a green olive-colored truck full of black asphalt. Oily heat drifted from the truck over the body and onto me. Two men in dusty blue clothes looked at the prostrated man and smoked an unfiltered cigarette, passing it back and forth like a joint as they poked the body with their cement-crusted shoes. Then they climbed into the truck and backed away from the body and drove down Lomonosova. What was going on here? Another corpse?

Armenian shop assistants from a 24-*chasa* store stood on the opposite corner; a huge Georgian cook with thick eyebrows came out in his white cap from the Avla-Bar. After him came a waitress in high heels, her hair streaked blond on black, her lips glaringly scarlet. I wondered whether it was some boutique lipstick, such as Obsession (was there such lipstick?), or whether it was a lead-enriched Russian lipstick. Lead for some reason enhanced color; old Hungarian paprika gained its startling redness from it. It seemed strange, and yet perhaps not so strange, that lips would carry the element of a bullet on them to appear bloody and seductive. Why is the color of fresh blood attractive? The waitress gingerly walked over to the body, flipped it over on its back, and dragged it off the pavement, perhaps to spare it from potential traffic. She dropped it next to the elevated pink-stone sidewalk. Then she kneeled astride the body and pumped its chest with her palms and slid up the torso and blew her breath into its mouth. I couldn't avoid noticing in this emotionally taxing and alarming moment that her miniskirt wasn't fully zipped. I wondered whether she was Russian or Georgian.

I contemplated the possibility that my life would pass and I would have never slept with a Russian. There were many other more meaningful and painful omissions (such as that I hadn't developed a perfectly healthy body or bought real estate in Istria), but this one struck me as the most immediately deplorable.

You can never draw conclusions from appearances. You would imagine that a Georgian cook with a barrel-sized belly would be more likely to be big-hearted, but he only flicked the butt of his cigarette across the street onto a parked black Lada before struggling back into the bar. The waitress pumped the athletic body for about three minutes and stood up in exasperation, cleaned the dust off her knees with her palms, and walked back to the restaurant. If this hadn't revived the healthy-looking corpse, nothing would—that must have been the general conclusion. Everybody walked away. The traffic continued as normal, and the young man lay in the street, face up, his lips scarlet with her lipstick.

What is the 911 number in this country? I wondered. Maybe I should call? Oh, surely someone called. Every country has its own way of dealing with the dead, and Russians have had enough practice; they should know what to do.

I walked past a billiards bar, which looked like the Van Gogh painting with all the green and the reddish, caviar-eyed, drunken players, and beyond the bar at the street corner I saw a dozen people gathered around the corpse. At least four hours had passed, and nobody had picked him up? A long-nosed woman in a black fur coat leaned over the body, lifted the young man's head in her left arm, and kissed him, angling her face sideways so their noses wouldn't collide. Then she set him down gently, but his head still produced a thud on the pink granite, and another woman who was weeping knelt and kissed him in the same manner, while seagulls flew above and shrieked, as though they were vultures caught in the pristine bodies of sailing birds. The second woman dropped the young man's head a little less cautiously, and it thudded, louder than the first time, on the marvelously thick granite.

Who were these women? Lovers? Sisters? With Russians, who kiss on the lips unpredictably, it's hard to tell.

So, the abandoned young man was developing a good social life, perhaps a better one than he'd had while alive. Will it become a fashion now for expensively dressed ladies to stop and kiss the handsome corpse? The corpse looked like a New Russian, a rejuvenated Anatoly Karpov with boney and intelligent features, but buffed up, fed, not so high-strung (as Karpov was after being skinned alive by Kasparov). His prosperous looks seemed enviable and were perhaps the cause of his death. But was he dead? He looked too good for someone dead so long. I thought that maybe this was all being filmed out of a parked car, a reality TV show for the city audience to laugh at the ridiculous callousness of current Russia. In that case, the actor was a good one, staying limp so long, reacting to nothing, not even to concussions. There was no blood around him, no bullet holes. Maybe he died of a heart attack? Or the truck killed him, and the blood was all internal. How come rigor mortis hadn't set in yet?

In the gateway of my apartment building, before the yard full of puddles which now after the rain reflected the moonlight, shivered a drenched tabby cat. Drops of water sparked off her. She didn't run away when I approached her but sneezed. I knelt by her and petted her, and she continued to tremble.

—What is it? I said in Russian, as though she'd understand it better than English. I picked her up and carried her home.

In the vestibule, the resident black cat hissed at her, and she attempted to flee out of my grip. Even in my room, she was so terrified that she hid in my boot and wouldn't come out till the morning.

Her eyes were full of pus. She purred as I petted her and cleaned her eyes with paper towels. Her ears were long and pointed and hairy on top, and her fur, somewhat striped, gray and black, had black spots as though she were a black-and-white photo of a snow leopard. She sniffed at the herrings I placed on the floor. Maybe they were too strong for her in this state. I offered a teacup of milk. She licked a little, looked at me, purred, and then sneezed, with milk flying out of her nostrils. I warmed her up with a blow drier from a yard away, and she purred incessantly. In Russian, purr is mur and so I called her Murmansk, after the city.

At a kiosk pharmacy, I bought antibacterial eyedrops, and later I took her to a vet, where she got deworming medicine. The vet opened the little jaws and pushed a pill with her thick finger into the throat and Murmansk swallowed. Since Murmansk was only about five months old, the vet delayed fixing her for three months.

Murmansk purred into my ears before sleep, telling me in her language that this was a beginning of a beautiful friendship. It's a strange thing how a big mammal and a little mammal can make friends.

On the way home, young women smiled at the kitten in the pet carrier and by association at me, which was a new sensation as usually nobody smiled at me in the streets. In a ground-floor apartment, an orange cat pawed at the window as though to get out to chase my kitten. Cats are almost universally beloved in Russia. You could see pictures of Gorbachev and Brodsky with their cats. Silly to generalize, but it strikes me that democrats are more likely to love cats than dogs as you can't rule a cat. Dictators love obedience, so no wonder you see pictures of Hitler and Tito with their German shepherds, Putin with his black Labrador, Stalin with terriers, although of course it's unlikely that he loved anybody. Stalin had dogs trained to run at the German tanks with explosives to blow up themselves and the tanks. Lenin, by no means a democrat, however, loved cats and there are a few pictures of him with his fluffy pet. Churchill said, *I am fond of pigs. Dogs look up to us. Cats look down on us. Pigs treat us as equals.* Anyhow, I was happy I would live with an anarchist, the kitten.

CHAPTER THREE

A pleasant encounter becomes a vague threat

NOT TO APPEAR TOO EAGER, I waited till the following day to call Masha. I heard typewriters clicking in the background. She suggested that we meet on top of the Vanity Building that afternoon after her work.

Masha's being late didn't surprise me. I mused on the perpetually bad traffic despite so many broad streets created for triumphal armies returning from Sweden. (Peter the Great designed the city for unfriendly relations with Sweden, which perhaps explains why so many well-nourished Russians looked like Swedes).

A couple of fit men with crew cuts—a bit on the heavy side, probably from too much weightlifting and vodka shots, impeccably dressed in three-piece suits—walked up and down the street.

My phone rang. —Are you on street? Masha asked. —Better wait upstairs on top floor. I shall be twenty minutes late.

I climbed the stairs, floor by floor, through Vanity Fashion. The kind of shirt you buy at TJ Maxx for twenty bucks was 26,000 rubles here (more than a thousand bucks). High-heel shoes, 42,000. This reminded me of a joke: a successful young Russian runs into a colleague and says, *What a wonderful shirt you got! How much did you pay for it?* Fifty dollars at Gostiny. *What an idiot, you could have got it for one hundred across the street!*

When I reached the roof-top restaurant, I was seated on a sofa overlooking the Khazan Cathedral. Masha showed up while I was finishing my second glass of red Saperavi. I stood up and kissed her left cheek and she pointed with her finger to the other. I kissed the right cheek, and she pointed to the left cheek again.

—What, are we going to be kissing all afternoon? I asked.

—Ah, you Americans, you need to learn! You don't know how to kiss. You must kiss three times, like the sign of the cross.

The Kazan cathedral dome reflected orange—the color of young copper—and blinded me for a moment. Masha took off her sunglasses.

—It's funny how fresh and shiny the copper dome looks now, but in ten years it will be all green and mossy like the old part of the roof, I said.

—How is that funny?

—Just strange what oxidation does to copper. Anyhow, where are you from?

—What do you mean?

—What do you mean by *what do you mean*? It's a normal question, you know. Like what city in Russia?

—Why Russia? Ukraina, Kharkiv.

—Why are there so many people from Ukraine everywhere?

—You try living in Ukraina and then you know.

—I run into Ukrainians everywhere.

—There are fifty million people in Ukraina. Why not complain when there are so many people from Germany everywhere?

—How do you know I don't? Anyway, you answered from an office?

—Travel agency. It doesn't pay. Nobody comes to office to buy billets—all online now. And for me it's hard, I must help my daughter go to school, get her good clothes, food, books.

—Where is the father?

—It's sad history. He trained with the Klitschko brothers. Professional boxer, killed.

—Boxing is a dangerous sport.

—Somebody shot him on street in Moscow. He was paid to lose fight, but he knocked down other man before he could pretend that he was knocked. Possible that other man also was paid, and he acted like he was knocked down, and did it first. Looked like husband didn't do his side of deal, and so was shot. Many bullets.

She sniffled. Her glaring red lipstick was melting and spreading over the natural margins.

—Did you know he was involved in that kind of dealing?

—*V Rossiya*, in those days, that was only way to live decent.

—Sir, would you like another glass of Saperavi red? asked the waitress who looked like Nicole Kidman, only taller and more beautiful, with sharp black eyebrows.

—*Da, konyeshna*, I said.

—You speak little Russian? Masha asked. *Meni nravitsa se eto*, she said.

—Really? You are prettier.

Masha laughed, and I realized that I had misunderstood her as saying that she liked her (the waitress), while she meant, I like it that you speak Russian.

—If you like her better, walk with her.

—I don't think I have enough money to take her out.

—And you have enough money to drink with me?

She gave me a look from the corner of her eyes, while tilting her head to exhale an impressive gust of smoke.

—Barely. This is a pricey place.

—This?

—Well, yes, twenty dollars for a glass of wine.

—But that's normal.

—In London, yes.

The waitress came back with a glass of Georgian red.

—I think I will drink another glass of chardonnay, Masha said. —Why are you drinking Georgian wines? California wines are better.

—I want to taste the Georgian varieties because I am thinking of getting into the wine import business in the States.

—You businessman?

—That would be overstating it. I used to be a banker.

—Early retired?

—Not exactly.

—It's *chut-chut* cold here! Goosebumps appeared on her forearms. —*Dyevushka*! she shouted to the waitress and asked for a wool blanket. The waitress wrapped us in blankets. Masha tightened hers around her neck.

From behind my back erupted a startlingly loud recording of Hitler's strident speech at Nuremberg. I turned around. A serious-looking man in a three-piece suit shouted, *Da? Slushayu!* into a thin blackberry and the rally speech quit. So that was his ringtone, just like the cop's in the car? A sense of humor, or a statement of political sympathies, or simply a practical choice so he'd never be confused about whether it was his phone.

She took a large sip, and when she put down the glass, the glass carried a clear print, with little vertical breaks in the red, above the swaying transparent green-yellow liquid.

She waved to someone. I turned around, noticing a hefty-looking guy with a crew cut in a black suit, red shirt, and a yellow silk tie.

—You know him?

—Peter is small town.

—Who is he?

—Do you need to know?

—No. It's just funny that he's dressed like the German flag.

—Horosho, where do you stay?

—In an apartment on Griboedova, opposite from the Russian Museum.

—Expensive?

—Considering what a dump it is, yes, it's way too expensive.

—How much?

—Do you need to know?

—I live far near Park Pobedi. She looked at me as though to emphasize the injustice of it, that she, such an elegant lady, should live in the Lumpen-proletariat section of the city, and I, a slob in generic sneakers with a creased blue shirt, in the very center.

I was close to finishing my drink. There was still a sip-worth left at the bottom. As soon as I put down the glass, the waitress lifted it and carried it away. I wanted to say, Wait, that's my drink, but I didn't, and only gazed longingly after the quickly receding silhouette carrying the glass, through which the setting sun reflected from the cathedral copper.

—Crazy how they take away your glasses here even before you are done, I said.

—At restaurants, you may not be quite done with your meal, and they already want to take your plate away. Are they scared people will steal the plates and the utensils?

—You are fast drinker! Are you so fast at everything you do?

—No, for example I am very slow with this.

I put my palm on her hand. It was surprisingly ropey, her long fingers continuing in delineated tendons.

—May I kiss you? (Guess who asked.)

—Do you need to ask for permit?

—Well, I don't want to be pushy.

—Maybe if you didn't ask you could. Would be natural. Now not spontaneous.

—But you just said…

—You not need to talk about something like that. Maybe Americans talk crass like that.

—Is it going to happen?

—I see. David?

I expected a question, but none came. —Yes?

—I am calling you.

—That doesn't make sense. I am here.

—You want sex?

—Well, a kiss for sure.

—Let's not pretend. Men will kiss but that's not what they want, they want sex. You want?

—Well, if you want to put it so bluntly.

—What does bluntly mean?

—See, we are having an English tongue lesson.

She put her hand on mine, like a card trumping another. —David, are you ready to spend three hundred dollars?

—You would do it for money?

—I will not do for nothing.

—I don't want to pay for something that I could get for free.

—You could? You could?

She leaned away from me and measured me up and down and petted my potbelly.

—Maybe if you knew how to dress.

—I give you compliments, and you insult me? Why didn't you say you wanted to do a trick? You could have saved us both a lot of time.

—A trick? We aren't circus.

—Well, we spent three hours together, we talked on the phone, you could have asked me to pay right away. It's not a very efficient way of working, is it?

—I am not working. I didn't know that's what you want. And I am shy. I thought maybe you want to be friend, and I shall teach you Russian, but now I see you don't want friend. *Ladna.*

—Are you disappointed?

—It's hard to find true friend. You not true friend. And it's getting dark, so you tell me if you pay.

—Two hundred is too much. Maybe one hundred.

—Who said two hundred? Where do you think you are?

—It would be less in Holland.

—You not in Holland. And their women not so pretty. I make you deal, 5,000 rubbles. You have?

—Sure.

—Before I go with you, show.

—OK.

—Why don't you give it to me? Don't you love to share? I share everything with my friends, bread, wine, apartment.

—I'll give it to you later. Isn't that the usual thing? I've never done this, so I don't know.

—I don't know what usual is. Who do you think I am?

—Isn't it obvious?

—I never do this, but you are friend.

—You just said I wasn't.

—I give you another chance to prove you my true friend, and you can give five thousand to help.

—Later.

—You not trust?

—I don't know you. What's the point of talking about trust before we get to know each other?

—I don't know you and you want sex. How can I trust man like that? You want to be friend, you have to help. You want success, you must trust in yourself. And even more important, in friends.

—No matter what, I must pay?

—If you don't pay, I don't know what happens.

Is she threatening me? I have to pay now because I've talked with her. Are some of the men around working with her?

—OK, I will give you one hundred dollars.

—But that's less than 3,000 rubble, only 2,600.

—Let's not put down the dollar, 2,650 is more like it.

—David, you are rich, how can you worry about little rubbles? My daughter and I are poor, and we need rubbles.

—Rubles, you mean.

—Yes, Rusky rubbles. My phone is out of minutes, that's why I couldn't talk with you longer. And I need to call daughter.

—I am not here to just give out money.

—How can you be such? You tell me you are banker, and you have many money. And that is not many money. Shall you borrow me ten thousand?

—When would you return that?

—Five days.

—I'll give you five thousand.

She took five crisp blue notes and put them in her purple imitation crocodile skin purse, which snapped shut like a crocodile mouth snatching a family of poisonous blue tropical frogs.

—We can go now. David, you want to go, we go.

—To my apartment? Or yours? Mine is closer.

—First, I need to top off my phone so I can call daughter.

I covered the bill and tipped twenty percent.

—David, that's too much tip. You like her better than me?

—That's a habit. We tip twenty percent in New York, so why not here?

Out in the streets, Masha said, —Let me first walk into Office Pub.

—You want another drink?

—I have to return debt, and now I can. I am so glad. I, I don't know what would happen if I couldn't.

—Should I go in with you?

—It's better they not see you.

Is she making it up, about these men, just to psyche me out? Is she a gambler feeding her habit by pretending to be a call girl?

After about ten minutes, she came out of the English-style pub; it even sported a red-painted English phonebooth in the front. Masha fluffed up her hair with her right hand and said, —*Ladna*, and now we can walk to *priyem platezhei*.

—What is that?

—Where I top off my phone.

We walked out and turned left and I almost stumbled over the body of the young man, back in the original supine position, his feet in the direction of the cathedral. His black shoes looked like concert shoes. He had grown a bit paler despite his five o'clock shadow in the meanwhile, but his lips had grown redder. He was in the shades of black and white other than his scarlet lips and a lip print on his cheek.

—This corpse has been here for at least eight hours, I said. Why doesn't anybody move him?

—They will.

—Who are they?

—What's rushing? It's over for him.

—Why doesn't an ambulance or a morgue car come to pick him up?

—Why ask me?

—Well, you are from here, sort of. Why wouldn't I ask you?

—If nobody touch him: mafia.

—He's too thin to be mafia. And his hair is too long. And they are touching him plenty.

—You know how they used to call Jeep Cherokee which mafia men drove? Shirokee! Wide. They didn't know how to pronounce it, so they said Cheap Shirokee! Cheap and wide.

—So you think he's a mafia guy.

—I know many mafia, and they come in all shapes. Thick, thin, long, short. . .

—I didn't know mafia was still around. I thought it was oligarchy now.

—Oligarchy is passé.

—Who is it now?

—Putin's cabinet and the new Russians. But the others are still here. Yes, there's oligarchy, mafia, communism, fascism, and the Czar is back, his bones, at Petropavlovsk.

—Wonderful, isn't it? With all the layers of history right here, there is no rush to pick up the corpses. What is one more or less in the city which had a million of them? And where are policemen when you need them?

—I need them?

—The dead man needs them.

—He doesn't.

—Where were they when he did?

—He never needed them. Nobody needs them. If you see them, dear David, cross the street to other side. Better not talk to them. The White Nights are coming. They must be good during the tourist season, but before it, they need to make money, so they are aggressive.

—What do you mean?

—Here's my phone store, I am going to top off.

—I can come in with you.

—Better not.

—You are coming with me right after it, so why split up?

—You don't trust? David, that is your problem. I shall call later, and if I don't tonight, I shall call Wednesday.

—Wednesday? I was paying now for now.

—We never said when. It could be tomorrow or in five days.

—You are telling me you are backing out of the deal?

—What deal? I didn't say I do anything. You are friend, nice man, helping poor Ukrainian. Shall see you in five days.

—You know people in the shop?

—Maybe. How would I know if I know?

—Now you sound like Donald Rumsfeld.

—Would I know him?

—You just might, at this rate. That would be a known known, rather than unknown unknown.

—Keep talking if you like, but I am topping off my phone. What nonsense are you talking? Are you drunk?

—I am just quoting the U.S. Secretary of State. *There are known knowns; there are things we know we know. We also know there are known unknowns; that is to say we know there are some things we do not know. But there are also unknown unknowns—the ones we don't know we don't know.*

—Should I call the police?

—*You* threatening *me*?

She put her hands akimbo, laughing at me.

—I mean, about the corpse.

She stepped into the shop through the glass door. I walked away, furious for being such a dolt. Why didn't I read it right in the coffee shop? Had I been picked up by a mafia worker? But who was she? Just when I concluded she was a sex worker, she slipped away, evading sex. She is a decent scoundrel, posing as a sex worker. She outplayed me. Oh, it is better this way, nothing sordid happening. And I have better things to do—research the art scene, the wine business, maybe buy an apartment.

It was dark now, and the streets were shadowy. I was followed by shadows, mostly my own. As I entered the gate to the courtyard, I looked behind me: nobody at my heels in the incomplete darkness of the nearly white nights.

CHAPTER FOUR

I encounter a variety of Russian ghosts

THE NARROW ELEVATOR BROUGHT ME UP to the fifth floor, shaking with an ill-timed motor, and, through a hole in the rust-chewed iron floor, I watched the darkness below. The floor could fail and off I go, so much for this life. Cement particles floated and clogged my nostrils. It seemed the building's reconstruction business was a mummification process.

I entered my apartment and walked across the floor, which shifted, and the cupboards opened from the shaking of the flimsy floorboards and cemented reeds. Maybe it was one of those floors Viktor Shklovsky wrote about in *A Sentimental Journey:* during the winter of 1921, when people ran out of coal and wood to burn in their stoves, they burned books, and when they ran out of Pushkin and Tolstoy, they burned their floorboards. In some cases, a whole family with the remaining furniture would fall through to the floor below. This apartment seemed to have undergone such a treatment, and the linoleum floor and a few reeds and a bit of mortar and cement were slapped over to cover up some of the holes.

I lingered in a hot bath and scrubbed the thick skin that had built up on the soles of my feet from the excess of walking. I collected the garbage in the apartment—spent matches, a bottle of curdled milk, and three empty green bottles of Borjomi—the Georgian mineral water—and went downstairs.

Murmansk sneezed, her nostrils sprinkling. I gave her a herring, and this time she liked it and shook her head upward like a little wolf the better to swallow.

On the ground floor the black cat stood in the same spot, on the second stair, and stared at me with transcendental caution, his eyes fluorescing, as though he was responding to a different dimension, and something that was invisible to me was visible to him, an ultraviolet cosmos. Animosity radiated out of the exilic Egyptian deity in this land of darkness. —You are a paranoid antisemitic misanthropic xenophobe!

My jocular address to the cat had a history to it; the domestic cat was considered so evil that the Hebrew Bible and the New Testament don't mention cats because the cat was an Egyptian deity, an object of idolatry. According to the Islamic lore, however, Mohammed cut the sleeve of his shirt on which a cat was sleeping rather than to wake her up. He claimed to have learned the art of patience from his cat, Muezza, who should be treated as a mother. Well, there was nothing motherly about this cat. He hissed and followed me. Maybe he didn't want me to pick up any more strays, as he didn't want cats in his yard. Or, more likely, he was drawn to the smells of leftovers I carried.

I swung the bag of garbage into the closest container, and the bag produced a muted noise as it landed, rather than the usual bang of bottles against the iron. Something soft had absorbed the sound. I peered over the edge of the container and made out a human body. Perhaps it's a discarded mannequin from one of the fashion stores lining up Nevsky? Or a drunk? Or the corpse from Griboedova? How would I find out? Well, a drunk would have a normal temperature, and at worst a couple of degrees cooler than a sober man. A corpse dead for twelve hours would be chillier than that, and even chillier than plastic in cool weather. I touched the man's hand. Amazingly cold and elastic—certainly not gypsum. What process does that, what makes a body colder than the surrounding things? Maybe it's somebody else's corpse. Maybe there is no shortage of corpses in Russia. I would find out whether this was the Griboedova canal corpse if I felt the lipstick on the lips from the Georgian waitress's failed resuscitation attempt and from the series of lovers. I was reluctant, sniffing the smells of rotting cantaloupes.

The black cat leapt up silently, startling me, and teetered on the thin edge of the container, his hairs on end. His whiskers twitched as he bared his teeth while analyzing the wealth of smells. He jumped in and slinked to the face of the corpse and started licking its lips. I thought, There's whale cream in the lipstick, that's like fish, and for the cat, irresistible.

I put my thumb on the corpse's lower lip and swiped quickly, shivering, while the tomcat growled; it was cat food. The cat leaped at my hand and bit me. I withdrew the hand; it hurt but wasn't bleeding. The cat continued licking the lips. I checked my thumb; it was greasy. What was the corpse doing in my yard? The city is not small. Is this a coincidence? Does this have anything to do with me? How could it? And how could it not? I brought the thumb to my nose, and it smelled like a perfume, like Obsession. I had no idea what the damned obsession smelled like, but maybe this was it. It should have an undercurrent of death to it, beneath the sensational effusion of purple lilies.

I rushed away from the dumpster and realized I didn't have a sou, or rather, a kopek, on me and strolled to Citibank on Nevsky and inserted my blue Citibank card into the ATM mouth and withdrew three thousand rubles and three hundred dollars.

Two policemen stood on the curb near the bank. Should I tell them about the body dumped in my courtyard? They might find it strange that it was in my courtyard, plus didn't I rub the epithelium cells of that man onto my fingers? Oh, shit, haven't I just picked my nose with the same thumb? Yes, it smells like lilies. I sneezed. What the hell, now it's a bit late. The young man was clean but maybe had a cold or hepatitis. It was probably all fine. If you started to worry about every touch and contact you have with human beings, there would be no end to washing and fumigating and scrubbing. And what would the waitress say? She put her mouth, exhaled, inhaled, salivated into the dead man's mouth. Why be squeamish?

I walked along the canal admiring the huge toy-like cathedral, the golds and blues and reds all twirled around producing a giddy sensation. Just think of it, all in the name of two men, Christ and the Tsar, to celebrate the blood of both, to mix it, and to create an illusion of the divine monarchy and monarchial divinity. *Spas na krovi*, Salvation on the Blood.

In 1848, where the cathedral stood now, Mikhailov, one of the eight would-be assassins, had thrown a grenade that missed the Tsar and exploded. The Tsar stepped out of his coach worried about his horses. The horses were all right. Then he examined the wounded guardsmen, and realizing that nobody was dead, he exclaimed *Slava bogu!* Praise the Lord! Grinevitski shouted, Will you thank God for this too? and threw another grenade, and the explosion was so powerful that it killed not only the Tsar but also Grinevitski. Nearly seventy years later, seven would-be assassins followed the same plot in Sarajevo in a highly successful plagiarism. Of course, Grinevitski couldn't sue them for the theft of ideas. The first would-be assassin threw a grenade and missed but the grenade wounded several pedestrians. And later, Gavrilo Princip succeeded, with a gun. And there are fresh corpses now, I thought. How awesome. Awesome in the original sense of the word: terrifying.

Absorbed in the wonder of walking through history, I passed by a small police car—blue and white, no cops inside, but in the backseat lay two black submachine guns. I leaned in to catch a better glimpse of the guns. Metallic, casual, obscene. The cops I had just seen outside Citibank accosted me.

—Your document, said one.

I was hoping they were not talking to me. They were not looking at me but they were standing in front of me.

—Document, document! You don't speak Russian?

—I speak Russian.

—*Davay!*

—I haven't done anything.

—You looked into our car.

—No, I didn't look in. I am just passing by, looking for a place to buy Pepsi.

—No Pepsi in car. Document!

With a trembling hand, I pulled out my passport.

—Americanets?

—Is that a crime, to be American?

—Your registration.

—It's in my apartment.

—You must have it on you. When did you land?

—Here, it says Pulkovo Dva, see.

I pointed with my thumb. The cop shone his flashlight over the passport, and I withdrew my thumb. It did seem reddish.

The policeman staggered and burped.

—You look at it, the cop said to his partner, and the partner said to me, —Lift your hands behind your head. Yes, like that.

He frisked me and with his hands in my pockets, he paused. He felt my ass like it could hide something.

—Where are you staying? Hotel Europa?

—I don't have that much money.

—You don't? Where then?

—In an apartment.

—What address? Dom?

—I don't remember.

—How get home when you don't remember?

—I know how to get there.

—You are like dog? You sniff your way around?

—Sure. Each street here has its own smell. Some smell like gasoline, some like coffee, others like fresh bread, stale basements. Mine smells like the canal, dead frogs, and wet newspapers.

—You don't know where you staying?

—I do.

—Where is your address, print?

—In the apartment. I have the lease agreement there.

—Where? What street?

—Well, right here, on the embankment Griboedova, in the next building, on the fifth floor.

—Show me keys. You want to invite us home?

Then he said to his partner in Russian to return the passport to me. The partner put the passport into my hands. It was wet now. How did it get wet? The cops sneezed in unison. One of them shouted, —*Otpuskayu*! You are free to go!

They staggered away. I was relieved they hadn't noticed my red thumb. I felt my pocket. Empty! The cops were running to the car. I should run after them and ask for my money. Now how likely is it that they would return it? They could push me into the car. I should write down their license plate number to file a complaint. A complaint to whom? The police? The embassy? How would I prove that this has happened?

The day hadn't started all that well; I'd already blown six hundred dollars. I took the first entry to the courtyard leading to my apartment, just opposite from the three containers of garbage.

In front of the container with the corpse, a Jesus was standing in shining black shoes and laughing joyously, and another drunken Jesus was trying on the jacket, while the third one was stripping to put on the shirt, and the fourth one was trying on the white underwear. So, they stripped the corpse.

The elevator wouldn't work. I walked up, admiring how worn the granite stairs were, indented and slippery in the middle from millions of steps, causing the stone to erode, the way a waterfall would, but then, considering the Russian talent for huge neglect, there no doubt used to be flash floods from various bathrooms and broken pipes, veritable waterfalls cascading down. As I puffed to the fifth floor, there stood a well-combed family of three, Father, Mother, and Son. They all sported shiny black hair and thick groomed eyebrows, and the father bore a canny resemblance to Stalin, with his powerful mustache. There was a catlike sleekness to all of them. They ignored my feeble greeting and passed noiselessly like self-conscious ghosts, stepping so gingerly over the dust-softened cement that they seemed to levitate in a thick mummification cloud.

In my refrigerator I noticed an uncapped and half-finished bottle of vodka, which now seemed an appealing measure. One whole bottle would be dangerous, but half would trash me just enough to forget, Russian style, that I was in Russia. After half a bottle, many Russians might forget they were in Russia. What, I am no longer loving being in Russia? There's truth to that, I thought, and placed the bottle on the table, and stared through the clear liquid, which didn't look threatening or promising. It looked like nothing, and yet, clearer than nothing. The liquid added a certain washed clarity, such as air after a storm.

My love of Russia was an illness, a self-destructive vortex. The evening should have been enough to inoculate me against Russo-philia, which sounds like hemophilia—once you start bleeding in any connection with Russia, you might not be able to stop.

I gulped vodka, and suddenly I felt clear-headed. Until now I had been in my prolonged insomniac haze, and all the events seemed surreal, but now normalcy was returning and even my sight improved. (This reminded me of a scene in *Radetzky March*. A myopic doctor, nervous before a duel, drinks half a bottle of Hennessey, and suddenly he can see everything in sharp detail. And he dies in the duel.) Vodka put my situation in a different perspective. A little introductory sacrifice to get to know a place, an entry visa, so to speak, was not bad. In the ancient times, I'd probably make a burnt offering to a god to be received in a friendly way. I'd have to burn a goat, cook it just right, so God might want to eat it. And the goat would cost—in current terms—perhaps just as much as I'd burnt in my missteps in the city of potholes.

I couldn't sleep so I walked aimlessly past the Konyushennaya square. Bottle shards glittered in the dark all over the pavement. I walked along the arcaded row of buildings, away from the sharded curb, along the walls. The cobbles below the arches were uneven, and some of them slippery, and all sorts of nocturnal creatures crouched there, with their bottles, which could be used not only for drinking but for smashing over people's heads. I had an uneasy feeling passing by the thick walls and crooked gates on rusty hinges with courtyards gaping and emitting smells of uncollected and burnt garbage and dead cats. I saw no police down the block and didn't know whether that was good or not.

It was a dark dawn, four thirty in the morning. The sky was intensely dark blue with a few whitish clouds; there was a pastel haziness and luminous depth of color above the rooftops. I gazed into the indigo infinity, and my eyeballs felt cool, bathing in the outdoor air without nicotine, without the steam of dancing bodies and spilled beer.

There was a row of bars and clubs on one side of the block, and on the other, two-hundred-year-old horse stables made of stone walls forming a majestic circular building. When all these bars and clubs spat out their drunken young just before dawn, with the sky paling, bottles were shattered against the walls. A few men were leaning against gate posts and vomiting. A pack of dogs was licking and slurping the vomit. One dog stumbled alongside me, either blind or drunk, quite unsteady, yet apparently in need of affection. Was it possible that even strays in Peter were alcoholics?

I crossed the street from this unholy sight of nightclubs to a holy one, the Blood Cathedral. In the opening behind the cathedral and before Mikhailovskii Sad, a pack of dogs—who looked like coyotes or mix wolf and yellow dog, all looking alike, an incested extended family or not so extended—was fighting ferociously. Ten dogs were encircling two, who fought valiantly. The pack took bites out of the two, and the two bled and yelped and bit back. The howling and the biting seemed normal to a few clubbies who stumbled across the bridge of another canal toward the Fields of Mars, with the flames to the unknown soldier flickering pink in the distance. In the field there were thousands of people buried beneath blank gravestones—thousands of unknown soldiers.

I didn't know how to help the besieged dogs and deemed it safer to walk away rather than to get involved in the yelping. Now it was a blue dawn above the rooftops on the cathedral steeples and on the street level it was still a bleak night. A flock of crows was attacking the garbage container in the yard. They were probably tearing at the remains of the young man. Now it would be impossible to know whether there had been cannibalism in the yard, or whether I had imagined it. Out of curiosity I walked to the container. Crows flew close to my head. What if they had developed a taste for human flesh? I leaned over, and among the garbage of all stripes, I saw a skeleton, some bones clean white, others pink and red. The wind created by the hungry birds smelled of wet feathers and honey.

CHAPTER FIVE

My landlady loved a German soldier

ANOTHER MORNING, I went to the Prokofiev café—although Tchai-koffski was an even better name for a café—and read on the internet and in *St. Petersburg Times*. One of the main distributors of Georgian wines was run over by a truck on Lomonosova just a couple of days after a Georgian importer was killed in a hit-and-run accident on Liteny.

Why do they call it an accident? I wondered. Bullets were suspect, but cars? If they kill someone, well, of course it's an accident. Car accidents were one of Stalin's favorite forms of execution. In Serbia, presidential candidate Vuk Drašković was recently targeted by a car and heavily injured. Was car as assassination coming back in fashion in Russia?

Next, I googled the name Griboedov because of the Embankment. Literally, it should mean Mushroom Eater but obviously mushrooms couldn't grow out of the cement and granite stones. I googled the playwright Griboedov and found out that he was as famous for his death as for his life. He had died in Persia, the kind of death reserved for privileged Americans, in an embassy siege. As Russian ambassador in Tehran, he received three persons seeking refuge, a head eunuch who had managed the Shah's personal treasury and harem, and two concubines from the harem, all of whom wanted to return to their native Armenia.

A rumor had spread through the city that the Russian infidels were defiling Muslim virgins. A rabble of furious worshippers broke down the gate; the Cossack guards and Griboedov fought the mob for more than an hour on slippery marble floors overflowing with blood. To save his life, Griboedov gave up the refugees. With their beautiful sabers, several men immediately cut the eunuch to pieces. They dragged Griboedov out of the building and beheaded him, alongside a few of his staff members. The rampage crew identified someone else's headless body as Griboedov's and dragged it through the streets of Teheran, rhyming insults, and then returned to the right Griboedov and continued to mangle him. The body, left in a pile of rubbish, could be recognized only by a scar on its hand, received in a duel. The duel had been part of the inspiration for Pushkin's *Eugenie Onegin*, and strangely enough, Pushkin accidently ran into the funeral party with Griboedov's remains on the way to Tbilisi. —What is this procession, he asked? —We are carrying your best friend's body to his grave, came the answer.

The Shah, to appease the Tsar, ordered mass executions of the mob leaders. The executions went out of hand, with soldiers randomly shooting nearly a hundred men. The Shah gifted the largest diamond in the world to the Tsar, and it's still on display at the Hermitage, a wondrous gem refracting the light into rainbow colors, but no doubt, best of all, into the reds.

That is something, I thought. And there's a body in a pile of garbage right in my yard on Griboedova, being torn apart just like Griboedov was. Maybe he was a descendant? Griboedov's spectacular death attracted biographers, and I wanted to track down the book by Laurence Kelly, *Diplomacy and Murder in Tehran*.

After too much coffee, I took a boat ride for fun and research on the Fontanka, Niva, Obvodni Kanal, Moika, but not Canal Griboedova, which was too narrow and featured bridges much too low for a large boat to pass under. A tour guide with a crackling megaphone related historical facts connected with each segment of the journey. She pointed at a dilapidated palace opposite from the Letny Sad, summer garden, with broken windows and peeling mortar as the place where anybody caught eating human flesh during the Siege was hanged, and there were dozens of such hangings.

Of course, the true extent of cannibalism in the war is unknowable. Histories of that period blur, and people's personal reports are unreliable because of delusions induced by hunger, fright, and hypothermia. I read reports that there were fewer than one hundred certified cases of cannibalism, an unusually low number, considering the amount of people starving to death. Likewise, some analysts put the death toll from the Siege to 650,000 and others to 1.3 million, and most somewhere in the middle range. Dogs and cats were eaten liberally, however, and one story about an entrepreneur went like this: he sent his pack of German shepherds to eat the corpses on the front, between the two warring sides. Thus, with lots of exercise and nutrition, the dogs got to be big, muscular, and shiny, and they fetched good prices when sold as meat. This wouldn't be directly cannibalism, but indirectly, human-fed dog meat.

As a dilettante historian, I was attracted to strange stories, strange and soulful, of course. It was time to recover my Slavic soul, and what better place to do it than in the country most famous for soul, Russia?

But like nearly everything in Russia, the Russian soul was an imitation. In the early nineteenth century, Hegel, Shelling, and the

German Romantics evolved the concept of the German national soul, *Die Deutsche Seele.* The concept spread to Russia, and Gogol, who ostensibly had nothing but contempt for the Germans, used the term Russian soul, and it stuck. Could it be that the Russian soul was simply the German soul but chillier? Would there be the Russian soul without the concept of the national soul? Would there be Russian cruelty without German cruelty, on the dark side? And would there be Tchaikovsky without Beethoven on the bright side?

Interrupting such musings, my landlady Natasha called me on the phone and an hour later stopped by and informed me that a potential buyer from Moscow wanted to visit the apartment. I didn't have enough time to clean up the apartment.

—Ah, what filth! Natasha said as soon as she walked in. She took off her fur coat made from a forest-full of foxes and panted as though she had climbed the stairs.

—I am so disappointed in you, she said. And you come from the civilized West? Before you, a retired Swiss ambassador stayed here and when he left, the place was cleaner than before.

—Don't worry, I will wash the floors. When is the buyer coming over?

—You don't have to do that. Hire a cleaning lady. They are dirt cheap. You could have told me you needed one.

—How could I have told you when this is the first time I see you? An agent let me into the apartment. I didn't have your phone number.

—I was ill. To survive surgery in a Russian hospital, what blessing! If you need surgery, I recommend Switzerland. You could have tracked me down through the agency. And I see you are keeping a cat!

Murmansk meowed at her.

The landlady looked at the litter box, sniffed, and said, —*Za-paha nyet*! It doesn't stink. It's all right then!

—You don't mind I am taking care of a cat?

—Why would I? At least we won't have any rats, and the way you keep the place, they could live here very well.

—How much are you selling the apartment for?

—One hundred and fifty thousand euro, that's a great deal. I would charge twice as much if the apartment was renovated. You want to buy it? One hundred and fifty-one thousand for you.

—But that's more than the other guy is paying.

—That's the point. I can already get that much. You want it?

—Oh, no, I can't afford it.

—I see you have bottled water here. No wonder you can't afford to buy apartments; you throw away your money even on water. What next? You will be buying thin air?

—I read the warnings not to drink tap water here. And if I could buy clean air, I would.

—There's nothing wrong with our water. We have excellent filtering systems, she said, walked to the faucet, and drank a glassful. —Refreshing!

—Giardia, lead, E. coli…that's what I've heard.

—That was years ago. And that is foreign propaganda. Why does the world hate us? Can you tell me that?

—The world loves Russia, perhaps a little too much.

—This is the new Russia. Our boy, Putin, has made everything work again. Do you know my son used to go to kindergarten with him, and he came up here sometimes to look at my son's stamp collection? He bought my son's German stamps. You know, Volodya always loved everything German. Anyway, our water is the best and it's wonderful that it can just flow out of the wall. Do you know why my fingers are so knotty?

—No.

—As a ten-year-old during the Siege, I collected icy snow with my bare hands—for our drinking water. We put the snow in pots. I get a little pension as a survivor of the Siege. Do you know who visited me in this apartment? Comrade Stalin. He came after the war to talk with a few survivors of the Siege.

—What was he like?

—He told me many *shutky*. Here's one. *Wherever Lenin went, there were huge posters of Lenin, but none in Poland. He told the Polish communist party leaders, Next time I come to Poland, I want to see an image of Lenin in Poland. Lenin in Poland, remember that. And a year later in Poland he paintings of Trotsky making love to Lenin's wife. He said, Comrades, I told you, I want pictures of Lenin in Poland. Yes, comrade, that is what it is. Lenin is in Poland!*

—I just saw a man looking like Stalin here the other day.

—Do you know who died on the stairway here?

—How would I?

—A German officer. It is a sad story.

—I imagine that after the Siege you'd want a German officer to die.

—The Siege was not his fault. He loved Sankt Peterburg to death. When he enlisted he asked to be sent here.

—He volunteered to bomb the city!

—He'd read about the city—all the works of Gogol, Bely, history books. He collected postcards from here as a little boy and dreamed of visiting Hermitage and Petropavlovsk. And so during the Siege he dreamed of deserting so he could come over into the city, but he knew he'd be killed either by his side or ours.

—And he still did it?

—Every day he stood guard on the Pulkovo hills watching through his binoculars—the spires of the Admiralty and Petropavlovsk and the golden dome of St. Paul's cathedral and the blue dome of the Trinity Cathedral. And he longed to be here.

—But instead sent you missiles?

—After the war he was a POW, again within the viewing distance, and he kept gazing this way. He was so tall and handsome that when he worked in a truck factory—part of his prison work—he fathered many children with several Russian women.

Natasha took out a variegated cloth handkerchief and dabbed her eyes with it. In a wet voice, she continued: —After he was released, he was shipped straight back to Berlin, and it took him twenty more years before he could get a visa to come here. He was so excited and it was so cold, minus twenty, that his heart gave out. He'd just stepped on the stairs and dropped dead. Down there, on the stairs next to the elevator entrance.

—I knew that atrium was creepy.

—He was coming to see me. Oh, I shouldn't have told you the story. I will have a nightmare about him. Here, I have a picture of him. You want to see it?

—I don't.

—He sent me one before he visited, and I got him the visa.

After the landlady left, I thought, if this obsessive German maniac put so much effort into seeing the city, why wouldn't I persevere?

CHAPTER SIX

Clean bill of health in Russia is a tricky business

To GET A VISA exceeding a three-month stay, I needed to leave the country and apply for one at a consulate in Estonia or Finland; I also needed an HIV test. I started to obsess about whether I could have contracted the virus somewhere, from my dentist, for example.

I asked a friend of mine, Sam, who had stayed in Russia for more than a year. —Do you know an HIV testing center? A hospital?

—Are you crazy? Sam said. You shouldn't trust Russian nurses to draw your blood with recycled needles.

—Well, how else can I be tested?

—I know a doctor who can issue you a certificate for ten dollars. Here, I'll give you her email address and phone number.

—So where do I go to get tested?

—You can meet her on the platform of Senaya Ploshad (Hay Market), line number three.

—And she'd jab me with a needle there?

—No, man. She would just give you a piece of paper testifying that you are negative, provided you send her all the information, such as your passport number, DOB. No need to take any tests.

—But isn't that dishonest?

—No, it's Realpolitik. If the system is unfair, sometimes you must beat it. The test could be dangerous. Even if the needle is treated by being poked into a flame, it could still contain some virus inside it, which could survive the heat if the needle is not held in the flame long enough. You could pick up hepatitis, TB, even leprosy. And HIV.

—But if I gave her all that information, she could steal my identity.

—And what would she do with it?

So, two days later, I gave three hundred rubles to a silver-haired woman in a blue raincoat at the corner of Malaya Morskaya and Gorohovaya and got the clean bill of health. The peculiar thing about HIV testing was that one was more likely to get infected in St. Petersburg than nearly anywhere in the States. Every tenth man in St. Petersburg carried the virus, according to *The New York Times*. It was the US who should be asking people to produce HIV certificates to re-enter the country after living in Russia. Anyway, so tested, in corruption at least, I managed to obtain a visa to remain in Russia and to explore the Russian soul.

The soul, however, seemed a very cruel one. There were beggars lined up along Griboedova, and one particular beggar seemed very nice. His legs were cut off, but he never asked for money directly. On the other side of the canal, at the entrance of the Kazan cathedral, worked another beggar, with his legs and hands cut off. He had only stumps for hands.

The massive cathedral was built to accommodate the icon of Maria of Kazan. In the dark brown space illuminated by thin bent orange candles flickering and shivering, a choir sang without instrumental accompaniment. People lined up in front of the icon, crossed themselves, genuflected either onto one knee or briefly onto both, and kissed the image of a brunette, her head in a scarf tilted, a hand with thin fingers gently lifted. Some kissed her on the ear, others on the thin lips, some on the broad forehead. The poor Northern Mother of

God—would Jesus agree to be born in the frozen landscape?—had to withstand a shower of kisses and bacteria and viruses, and the people, while extracting a blessing with their lips, accumulated a wealth of potential diseases to succumb to or to pass on; on the other hand, under the divine auspices, perhaps this was a highly efficient system of inoculation against the identified and yet unidentified diseases. I gazed at the image, and wondered to what extent Mona Lisa was similar, or even borrowed from this one. Most of the recent Tsars had kissed this one, Rasputin had, Dostoevsky had; just one little kiss could give you both Russian spiritual and bacterial history. If I am to experience Russia, this is it—I should close my eyes and kiss the glossy and cracked canvas.

A choir of heavenly music cascaded from a balcony in decrescendo, ending in whispers. I was hesitant, like a boy about to embark on the first kiss, and I couldn't do it. It would mean nothing without faith, after all. Maybe no kiss without faith means anything.

I walked out of the cathedral into the glaring sunlight and gave a bunch of rubles to the two maimed beggars, suspecting that the beggars wouldn't get to keep the rubles but would have to give them up to a mafioso, who also probably had someone above him. It was a food chain, a business of exploiting the chemistry between misery and altruism.

Later in the day, I got together with the Sam at Kofye Hauz. I told him I was HIV free.

—You seem to be promiscuous, so I thought you'd be the right person to ask about taking the real test.

—Well, that was a good hunch, he said. —Last night a young lady invited me over to her place, and while we were making love, her mother banged on the door and shouted, Stop it in the name of Mother of God! Mom, we can't, we love each other too much. I beseech you to stop! came a shrill cry from the corridor. And the mother lit candles and prayed Pater Noster in Church Slavonic, and some other prayers I couldn't make out.

—How could you carry on?

—I guess we were drunk and culturally insensitive. By the way, I know a fine Armenian restaurant half a flight of stairs underground on Nekrasova, Stary Dom. You can treat me to a stew, can't you, since I got you the HIV passport?

After Zhukovsky Street, together with his Croatian friend Mario, we walked onto Nekrasova.

—Who is happy in Russia? I said.

—What do you mean? Sam said.

—Other than you? That's the title of a famous poem by Nekrasov.

—Funny how such a title wouldn't make sense in Hawaii, Sam said. There, you kind of have to ask, Who isn't happy in Hawaii?

—Never underestimate the human potential for misery.

—Who said that? Sam asked. Schopenhauer?

—Who'd have to say it? It's one of those truisms.

We made it to the restaurant and ordered lamb shashlik, lamb soup, and Georgian mineral water, Borjomi.

—Sorry, no more Georgian mineral water. The imports have ceased, said the waitress in a shiny green dress.

—Why? I asked.

—Don't you read the newspapers? Government food inspectors have determined that Georgian mineral water contains bacteria.

—And the Russian mineral water doesn't? What doesn't carry bacteria here?

—This water is safe.

She placed a green bottle of Russian mineral water on the table. A huge man with closely cropped hair, big eyebrows, and unusually closely set eyes came to our table, and said, —*Po chemu po angliski?* Why are you talking in English?

—Because we come from Canada, answered Sam jokingly.

—Canada? You could speak French.

—Ontario, not Quebec.

—And I come from the States, I said. Pittsburgh.

—And Mario said, I am from Croatia, but I study in the States, at Columbia.

—Colombia? Why not Venezuela? That Chavez is a fine president.

—That's the name of a university in New York.

—From Croatia? Why not Serbia?

—I was born there, and I like it well enough.

—Well, at least it's not Bosnia, the giant said.

—What do you mean? Mario asked. During the war Croatia was safer than Bosnia, for the most part, other than around Vukovar.

—At least you're not Muslim, that's what I mean. We have problems with them down in the south. I hope you killed some?

—I wasn't involved in any of that.

—There's a war and you stay away from it and let your people be killed?

—I was a teenager.

—Teenagers can make good soldiers. You like your country and do nothing for it. So what are you all doing in Russia? Why Russia?

—Why not Russia? Mario said. —It's the biggest country on earth. We are taking part in a literature conference with courses in journalism.

—Journalism?

The man, Sergei, pointed at Mario's temple with his index finger, imitating a gun to the head. —Puff!

I paused, not quite sure whether this giant meant that journalists should be shot.

—And literature? Sergei said. —That is even worse. I used to like it until I was fourteen, but then I had a Jew for a teacher, and that was enough to disgust me with books forever.

Sergei waved to his friend at another table, who looked raw as well, holding a debate with himself. If he debated with his own mind angrily, he'd certainly be even angrier with other people's minds. Maybe better to say nothing, I thought, so we can hear what people really think. *In taverna veritas.* Samuel, who was tall, lean, bearded, and looked pretty much like Jesus, which is to say, classically Jewish, seemed tempted to say something, but he too probably decided this would be a study. And who would want to fight a gorilla on his turf? What would be definable as victory? One should think of victory the American way: what's the exit strategy? How do we get out of here?

I asked, —What did his ethnicity have to do with your not liking literature?

—You can ask? You know the answer.

—No, I don't, unless you are an anti-Semite, and you assume that I am too.

—Anti-Semite? What kind of word is that? Who uses such words? Everybody is anti-Semitic. And the whole world is anti-Russian, and that's not a problem. See, that kind of thinking makes me angry, and that's why I didn't like that literature class. You Jewish?

—Not really.

—No wonder you won't drink!

—No, I just said not really.

—Prove it then, have a shot of vodka with a real Russian anti-Semite! Ha ha!

—I am not going to drink, and you can think anything you want of it.

Rainwater poured down the stairs and created a pool two inches deep. That didn't distract Sergei, who said, —Everybody in my family used to work for the KGB. My grandfather, my father, my uncles, they were all officers. I was the only one who was the common soldier for the KGB. You think there were no common soldiers for the KGB? You are wrong, *druzya*, wrong.

Now I wondered what being a field soldier for the KGB meant. Giving people concussions? Discouraging people from emigrating?

The water kept pouring down, thunder made the windowpanes shake, lightning flashed.

—Why aren't you drinking with me? How about *dveysta gram*? Two hundred grams.

—No, thank you, I said. I am a nonalcoholic. (I'd been on the wagon already for two days, which I counted as a huge accomplishment.)

—You don't drink? Against your religion?

—I don't have a religion. I just don't drink.

—How about you, he addressed Samuel.

—I don't either.

—You better drink with me.

—How so? Sam answered.

—You look like you don't drink enough.

—This is just my day off.

—What day of the week is it? Saturday?

—I don't keep track, said Sam.

—Don't you know who I am? Sergei asked.

—You told us, Sergei the KGB soldier, I answered.

—There's no KGB. Yeltsin got rid of it. I am an architect, an artist. You don't believe me? I'll show you my website with my original designs. If you want to build a dacha, just give me a call.

—But we don't live here, I said.

—That doesn't matter. If you need help, just call your friend Sergei, and I will be there. If anybody gives you trouble, I will smash his head.

—You are a nice man.

—I have a big Russian soul. And big fists.

Sergei wrote down my cellphone number in huge ciphers. Then he ordered two hundred grams of vodka for himself and sobbed.

He said, —Poor Milošević! You Americans killed him. He was the last good Slav.

—America has nothing to do with it.

—Yes, it was a modern style, biochemical assassination. He stood up against the Muslims, Sergei said. —We needed a president like that. If he'd been here instead of Yeltsin, we'd have no problems in Chechnya.

—But now you have Putin, Sam said.

—Yes, that's an improvement, said Sergei.

—Do you think Putin will be president for life? Mario asked.

—Of course, Sergei said. —He will be president for life.

—But what about your constitution? I asked.

—Constitution? That's a yellow piece of old paper. You can change it in five minutes, just type up another one.

Sergei moved to the table with his friend, swearing. Sam and I walked up Nekrasova; the downpour had ceased. For a street named Not Pretty (in translation), it was quite a pretty street, with gray stone buildings and red roofs.

St. Petersburg was built over millions of tons of rocks that had been dumped to fill in a swamp. Around a hundred thousand people had died in building the city within the first twenty years of laying the foundations and erecting the palace-like Italianesque monsters. People were buried right there. Their bones contribute now to the solid ground below the city, a hundred thousand skeletons, without crosses, names, just there to give the city its ghost-like aura. With the flooding, the smell of rot emanated out of many buildings, from the basements.

—Who is happy in Russia? I said.

The next day, perhaps to be happy as much as one can be while rooting for a team in soccer, I walked into the Tinkoff brew pub on Kazanskaya, to watch the World Cup Finals. To enter the brewery, I passed through a metal detector. —You have no guns? asked the guard. If you do, no problem, just leave them here. We had a shooting here last week, so now we have to screen.

—No, I don't carry a gun.

With his slow eyes, the guard measured me scalp to toe, apparently coping with the notion that there was a class of people that didn't carry guns. The huge bar was packed for the world soccer championship finals in progress on some twenty large flatscreens. I got a spot at the bar, facing a screen high up, which gave me a crick in the neck. I used to play soccer as a kid in Belgrade. Kids took soccer there seriously; they knew how to dribble and use all sorts of tricks; they ran fast, elbowed each other. Whenever I was assigned to a side, the side's captain complained that the team would be weakened, and so I got an inferiority complex as a soccer player, but nevertheless, I followed soccer.

Next to me sat two young women and one beefy guy, drinking beer in long gulps, growing redder and foamier.

—There's a special, I said to the guy. Two for one. You clearly plan to keep drinking.

—Of course, I will keep drinking. But I don't need any specials.

—You could save money.

—Do I look like I need to save money? He looked at me from above. —What's the matter with you? You are an American?

—Yes, in America even the rich save.

—Yes, but I think you aren't one of them.

He switched places with one of the women and she sat next to me. He put his hand on the shiny skin above her knee. She placed a thin brown cigarette into the ashtray. That reminded me of Masha, so I looked up. It was not her.

I glanced up at the screen. With the snap of his head, Zidane hit an Italian player in the chest, and the player went down. What marvelous vitality to react like that, to go headlong into an enemy! Did he premeditate the hit or was it instinctive?

After the game, I was leaning against a railing, dejected, with thoughts of my dead father, and dead men in the streets of foreign cities.

A Frenchman came over to me and hugged me and wept on my shoulder. —*Perdu!*

—I have other problems, I said.

The Frenchman looked at me in amazement. —But you look so sad, I thought you must be French.

Many people were abandoning tables laden with long sausages, kebabs, and pitchers of beer. Masha was gone.

On the way out, I grabbed a long sausage, which coiled like a poisonous snake angling to bite. It was spicy and good. In the mayhem nobody paid any attention to me—dozens of men in suits with disarranged ties, flushed from drink and shouting, wobbled through the doors. They seemed happy. Maybe this was a wedding party of the Italian and Russian Mafias? A perfect evening for them, not for me.

Outside, a stench. A man with a gangrene foot was sitting on the back stairs of the Kazan Cathedral. I gave him the rest of the coiling sausage, and the sick man blessed me. *Blagodaryu!*

I had been seeing and smelling this man for nearly a month. How was it possible that in a country so rich, with so much police, a man like this would be left in the streets? Shouldn't he be taken to the hospital and treated while it's still possible? What's to be done? All I could give the man was some food and occasionally a bit of vodka to wash his foot with.

CHAPTER SEVEN

I discover the delights of the Russian pharmacy

IN MY WANDERINGS over the fascinating city, I strayed into Luteran-skoye Kladbishche. This mostly German cemetery had been neglected; after the war, anyone with German heritage didn't dare go to the cemetery. Consequently, the cemetery was now an old growth forest with powerful roots penetrating the crypts. Some cement casings had cracked open, and white bones lurked in deep darkness. A pack of six orange dogs cruised and sniffed around the graves and here and there took a leak, perhaps to reserve the bones for a moment of real need. The dogs were quieter than the pack at Mikhailovsky garden as though out of respect for the dead, or, more likely, since this section of the city didn't contain many clubs, they were not drunk.

I thought about where I would die, and where my bones would be buried, and how, and would they one day resurface? A vein on the left side of my forehead seemed to be ticking and pulsing. Of course, a vein couldn't do that, it had to be an artery. Will I die of a heart attack? My father had, in Belgrade, where he was a deputy ambassador (rising in ranks from being the economic advisor), kind of like Griboedov in Persia. He and I had walked up the hill to the zoo. It was a sunny day, and I was eager to go faster; I'd heard the lions roaring. Let's go see them roar! My father huffed and panted, his face was covered in whitish sweat, as though flour had collected on it; he leaned against the muddy stone wall and slid. A long snore came out of his open mouth, a wet gurgling sound, and it kept coming out for almost a minute, and he did not inhale again.

The image of my father's grave, a cube of emptiness and green soil for the walls to that emptiness, disquieted me. I remembered how the casket was lowered down on thick ropes, thick enough to anchor a ship, and it sounded like the wood was being sawed.

A quiet dread nauseated me. I measured my pulse using the Nokia as a stopwatch, 120 beats a minute. Russian hospitals scared. I would feel better with American disinfectants around. I waved down a cab, and an Armenian in a brown leather jacket, who was drinking red wine from a bottle, drove me to the American Clinic near St. Isaac's Cathedral for one hundred rubles. He offered me a swig of wine out of a blue bottle, which I declined.

—It's good for your heart, he said.

—Yours must be excellent.

—No, it's terrible. Two glasses a day are good for you, but two bottles aren't. My heart is enlarged and lazy.

I rang the bell to the clinic and presented my American driver's license to be admitted. Once I walked in, I lost balance and while passing out, still managed to aim for a loveseat upholstered in fake yellow leather. I woke up on a table under glaring white lights. Where the hell am I? I looked at the walls and saw diplomas, which displayed the MBA acronym, and I wondered whether it was Russian, MVA, and what did it mean? Certainly not MD, nor a Master of Veterinary Acupuncture, but Master of Business Administration. This was in English and a B was not a V.

I jumped off the table and rushed out of the windowless room.

I bumped into a handsome blond man in white and green dressed as a doctor and shouldered him so vigorously that the businessman fell back against the wall. I leaped to the door, but the door was locked.

A secretary dressed in white came out and said, —You can't leave unless you pay.

—Pay for what?

—ER visit.

—I am not staying here unless you show me an MD diploma. Can you show me one?

—Of course.

—OK, I'll wait.

—I can't go into the ER room, it's locked, the doctors have an emergency, and there are the diplomas.

—Open the door or I'll call the police. This is a rip-off.

—We'll call the police for you.

—Go ahead!

—Please leave the premises, said the clerk.

I walked into the streets, suddenly feeling perfectly fine. The sunlight gleamed on the golden cupola of St. Paul's Cathedral, the sky was heavenly blue, and I was saved. No hangover, no nausea, nothing. I was glad I'd read the diplomas because who knows what treatment I would have got from my fellow Americans. What kind of trustworthy American would go to Russia to practice medicine? So, a serious financial threat may be the best cure for heart attacks, better than defibrillation. I should present it as a case study at the Mayo Clinic—one group about to have a heart attack for free, and another to pay out of pocket, and see which group has more heart attacks.

I walked past St. Paul's Cathedral, checked out the plaque where Pushkin had died protecting his wife's honor. Ironic, since it was his hobby to sleep with other men's wives, and he had slept with more than a hundred of them, allegedly. Wasn't that a bit hypocritical of him, to resent his wife and even more her lover for doing what he was doing as a habitual fornicator and adulterer. (As such, Pushkin, if alive and applying for American citizenship, would be denied! That is, if he truthfully answered the question, Are you or have you been a habitual fornicator? That's the second disqualifying question after, Are you or have you been a member of the communist party or another subversive organization?) I looked out onto the vast square, around which cars drove in tire-squealing arrogance.

My elation at avoiding a mugging in an American hospital didn't last. The American organized crime was so well organized that it was not a crime; it was actually a virtue to give thousands of dollars to American doctors, not only in America but everywhere. I felt my heart pound against my ribs, which seemed natural enough, but it was beating against my left shoulder blade as well. How could it push back there through the left lung? I inhaled, and it appeared to me that my breathing was wet, as though I had pneumonia.

I would not be an American if I hadn't dabbled in pharmacology and self-medicating. My citizenship could be revoked—which from the tax-paying standpoint wouldn't be all that bad, since even while living abroad Americans must pay taxes. Taxes—the very word added to my blood pressure. Have I paid my 2005 tax? Heavens, I was late. Maybe I should emigrate in Russia after all.

At a pharmacy on Canal Griboedova and Gorohovaya (close to where Rasputin used to live), I stared at the drugs on glass shelves. There was Viagra, the champion of spam discount emails. Things were not going so well that I'd need a blue pill, I reckoned, but only Lipitor or Zocor (simvastatin). I asked to see all the simvastatin brands.

—Do you have a prescription by a *vrach*? a bleached pharmacist asked me.

—No, but could I buy it?

—You really need a prescription.

—Well, I don't have one. I could get one, I am sure.

—Next time, come with a prescription.

—*Do svidanya!*

I turned around to walk away.

—This time, we'll make an exception. This one is the best; it's made in Germany.

I was surprised that she was still talking to me, and I turned around and came back to the glass-encased counter. —And this one?

—Nearly as good, made in the Czech Republic.

—This one?

—Not so good, made in Cyprus.

—And this one?

—I wouldn't recommend it.

—But why not?

—It's made in India. You never know how they work.

—But it's the cheapest, so could I have two packs, please.

—What? You want these? Did I hear it right?

—Yes, actually three packages.

—But I am warning you.

—What is this? You admire the Germans who nearly exterminated you, and you mind the Indians, who are the best engineers in the world. In fact, even in Germany now the best engineers come from India, and that's perhaps the only reason I would buy a German pill. By the way, do you have a statin made in Russia?

—No, believe me, you wouldn't want a Russian statin.

—But you have very fine engineers, you went into outer space first.

—We used to have them. Most of them moved to Germany.

The pharmacist called her assistant.

—Listen to what this man says, that Indians are the best engineers; could you repeat it?

—Indians are the best engineers in the world.

They sold me the three packs in a rush, to accelerate my exit.

When I got home, Murmansk celebrated with me, rubbing against my ankles while I prepared coffee, and then as I lay on my bed, she nudged her wet nose, sign of good health, straight into my left ear and purred and tickled me so that I laughed. Her purr vibrated comfort and assurance, in a slow steady pace, calming my heart. A cat is a natural pacemaker, which anybody in cardiac doubt should hold close to his chest. I believe I would have kicked the bucket in one of my anxiety attacks if Murmansk hadn't purred for me.

I read about the potential side effects of simvastatin. One, rare but sometimes deadly: muscle degeneration and atrophy, mostly in the legs, possibly leading to paralysis, and sometimes affecting other organs, such as the heart—resulting in sudden death. I took the simvastatin anyway, and to enhance it, some niacin. And naturally, I did all this with a triple cappuccino, never in the least blaming coffee for anxiety.

A few hours after reading the side effects litany, I experienced spasms in my calf muscles. When I walked on Nevsky, the weakness in my calves and dizziness made me gasp. Lou Gehrig's? That would give me only two years to live, max. Oh, here I am, thinking of all the dangers outside, but the greatest enemy is within, my own physiology and central nervous system. Now my anxiety mounted so much that I was both aware that I must be having a hypochondriac episode and that I was in ill health. You can have an illusion and be totally right at the same time and actually see what is there, not so apparent to others, and the illusion may amount to vision. Illusion is not necessarily a delusion. Yes, my cholesterol is high, my blood pressure is up, I have insomnia, arrhythmia, and it may all be a perfectly normal response to Russia, and in fact, may be a sign of an adequate hormonal response to the various provocations, allures, and threats on Nevsky.

I rushed to buy beta blockers at another pharmacy, also on Griboedova and Gorohovaya (Russia is like America in that respect, nearly every city corner featuring a pharmacy and a bar).

—Could I have some beta blockers?

—If you have a note from a *vrach*.

—I happen not to have a prescription, but I think my heart is beating too loudly.

—What do you want?

—A calming drug.

—We have tranquilizers for that. You know which one you want?

—Tranquilizers are mostly for the mind. My mind is fine; most likely it is. Well, you can never be sure about such things, can you? But it's my body that bothers me.

—Your body? Asked the platinum-bleached pharmacist.

She looked exactly like the pharmacist in the previous pharmacy, and maybe was. Did this woman also hate Brahmins and Sikhs?

—I recommend this one. Minimal side effects, very good for lowering blood pressure and establishing a steady heartbeat.

—How much is it?

—Three hundred rubles, fifty pills, fifty milligrams each.

—All right, I'll take it.

—Where is your prescription?

—I already said I don't have one.

—You must have one, she said.

She collected the money and handed me the pills.

I walked out and admired this concept of prescription. A prescription is a simple topic of Russian conversation when you get under-the-counter drugs. It is a reminder that you are swine, and that they are swine, and that everybody is corrupt, and that at the same time, it is a waste of time to visit doctors. And that it's much healthier to talk about them than to visit them. In fact, there's something accurate about this worldview. The difference between this and the American system: In the States you are denied the drug in the pharmacy unless you visit a doctor, who might refuse to see you next time, unless you buy the most expensive drug on the market, whose poster she or he has in illusory 3-D on the wall, always somehow resembling the DNA model. Yes, you must take Lipitor, my American doctor would say. The net result in either country is that you get whatever drug you want, but you pay more for it in the States in time and money, and in Russia, you pay only in self-respect, which, if you are a true Russian, you have lost so long ago that it is not a loss anymore but a reminder of what you would lose if you had it. In fact, it's a nice game, which, if you play it well, boosts your self-respect and confidence.

To hell with anxiety. Anguish is a fine word, better than the Latin and Greek roots of it, and better than the German Angst, which almost everybody pronounces as engst, which is another German word entirely. Anyway, I would get rid of my Anguish.

After I took the beta blockers, I did feel much better. Then I read that statins and beta blockers can interact adversely, paralyzing your heart in higher doses. I expected that would send me into another anxiety spin, but no—I didn't care. And so what if it happened? I might not notice but would pass out before death and wouldn't feel a thing.

I walked on Nevsky thinking of Kundera, feeling the lightness of being and since it was Kundera, it was pretentious, so saying unbearable would be redundant. (Oh, he's fine, but I just felt mean, and mean thoughts gave me an illusion of bearable heaviness of nonbeing.)

I felt good as I approached the Fontanka River. I never felt good around the Griboedova, as though the canal was poisoned, but as soon as I approached the Fontanka the world improved and the sky opened up. I walked behind a woman who seemed interestingly narrow yet curvaceous. She walked in a particularly springy way, despite her high heels, and her posture was magnificent. Clearly aware that I was looking at her while passing by her, she curled her lips. There was nothing inside me to worry about and there was this wonderful world outside filled with architectural and feminine graces. The beta blockers seemed to diminish my sense of existential uncertainty and threat. Strange to imagine that a whole philosophical movement, Existentialism, perhaps wouldn't have taken place if people had serotonin reuptake inhibitors and beta blockers, or perhaps there would have been no philosophical movements at all but more performance arts instead.

I looked back and talked without premeditation. —*Mozhna poznakomitse?* Can we be acquainted?

—*Mozhna!* Where are you from?

—New York.

—I always wanted to visit.

—You are invited.

—You don't even know me. How many girls have you invited to New York?

—You are the second one. Maybe the third.

—*Ladna.* Tell me your number.

She typed it in swiftly, and my phone vibrated in my hand and sounded its tango tune.

—There you go. Now you have my number. Call when you feel like it.

—I feel like it now.

—I am busy for an hour, a business appointment, but then I'll be free. *Menya zovut* Yuliya!

I watched after Yuliya and wondered. An hour's worth of business, what could that be? Why do I suspect? Of course, it could be anything. Why should a meeting go on any longer?

I called her the following day, and she said, —I could see you after five when I get off work.

—Work?

—In a big home supplies store. Russians are remodeling their apartments everywhere, good business.

CHAPTER EIGHT

The Russian art of imitation assumes many forms

YULIYA INVITED ME to an art opening at the library on the corner of Nevsky and the Moika. The theme was Dostoevsky and his influences on art. Half a dozen stooped and balding middle-aged men with beards smoked filterless cigarettes and milled about. Many paintings exhibited scenes from his novels; an axe, *topor*, attracted my attention.

Imitation seems to be a form of art in this city, which arose as an imitation of Amsterdam and Rome. So when Peter the Great introduced Western fashion, the Russians could outdo the Westerners in curtsying and other complex manners, and they can do so even now. In style, young Russian women outdo the models they imitate. If the models' skirts are short, Russians make them shorter; if the heels are high, they make them higher; if the jeans are low-cut, revealing the navel, Russians wear them even lower, and a strange thing happened—out of the excessive imitation sprang the Russian style, so now models in New York and Hollywood attempt to look like casual Russians, or like groaning Russian tennis players. If you imitate so well that you improve on the original, the original might imitate you.

The same thing happened with vodka, which was most likely distilled first in Poland. In imitating something foreign, Russians have managed to make even vodka drinking original. So if at the party people imitated Dostoevsky, they were doing the real Russian thing, creating doubles. Everybody in Russia should have a double, and in some way does, and while many people attempt to be Dostoevsky's doubles, it seems none succeed, other than in looks and debt. The amazing thing about Dostoevsky was that although he was a best-seller, he could never afford to buy an apartment, and lived in seventeen different ones. His wife, Anya, was intrigued why he couldn't save money and one day she got dressed as a beggar, hiding her face, and sat at the entrance of his habitual place of worship. As he crossed himself upon seeing the cross of the church, she said, *Kind Sir, could you give a kopek to the poor mother of two?* He gave her two rubles, which would be like two-hundred dollars in current terms. And she said, *Oh, so that's how our money goes, you give it away randomly!*

Here and there in the streets, I saw Lenin, Stalin, and other lookalikes. In a Russian gallery, I met a woman whose life goal was to re-enact every stroke of Van Gogh. She was halfway through his opus. If it's a musician's goal to play out every note Beethoven composed, why wouldn't it be a painter's goal to dab out every line Van Gogh or Rembrandt composed? (Wasn't Beethoven Dutch/Flemish, after all? What's *van* doing in front of his name?)

While it would be interesting to transcribe every line Dostoevsky wrote—it could also become insufferably boring—it's hard to imagine saying, *Let me write this line with more feeling. I feel more transcribing Dostoevsky than you do, and my lines are more graceful than yours; I am a better performer of Dostoevsky texts than you are. . .*

When *zakuski* were brought out—small slices of white bread with salami, butter, and cheese, and some with red caviar—the visitors to the exhibit attacked the tables and the food was gone in a matter of minutes. Russians could not resist free food; they devoured it as though it were still 1921, and they had no idea where the next meal would come from.

Yuliya and I walked to the Summer Garden, with all sorts of sculptures in white stone made whiter by pigeon droppings.

—Are you married? Yuliya asked.

—I am too old to be married. I am no good at performing husbandly duties.

—No, you are not too old. Only twenty years older than me, not a problem. My best friend married a German who is fifty-five and they are happy. They travel, have a child, and I plan to visit them.

We sat on a bench overlooking the Fontanka. I leaned over to kiss her but she evaded me.

—This is too fast, she said.

—How long should I wait?

—A month, minimum.

—If we marry, you will kiss me?

—If you marry me tomorrow at five, I will kiss you tomorrow at five.

—But how could you marry me if you don't know whether we can make love?

—It's easy to make love. Any idiot can do it.

—I would like a test.

—Good try, but no, without the marriage certificate, no go.

We went to Shatyor, a tent-like restaurant with live jazz. The pianist looked like an executioner, tall, boney, with sharp jaws, big eyelids, and overgrown connected eyebrows. I thought it would be more natural for this guy to take up a topor and to smash the piano into pieces in a couple of strokes than to sit down and play subtle melodies by Schubert, which he proceeded to do, displaying a great deal of gentleness and sensitivity.

We sat on a white upholstered loveseat and drank Riesling. She moved toward me and with her fingers removed the collar of my shirt, and said, —What is this?

—A mosquito bite which I scratched. My skin is sensitive so it's red. Maybe I should take Benadryl for allergies.

—Some loving mosquitos! It's a *zasos*.

—*Zasos*? I don't know that word.

—A love bite. Kind of what Dracula would do. What is it in English?

—A hickey.

—So how did you get your *zasos*?

—I told you already.

—Why would I believe you? A foreigner in this city usually ends up with a large hickey. We bite.

—I am not used to the poisons in your mosquitoes; I tend to overreact. Why the hell are there so many mosquitos in this damned city? I am shy and don't talk to women all that often.

—You talk to women on the bridges. That's not shy.

—Only on the Fontanka bridge.

When we walked out, standing in front of Hotel Europa, she laughed covering her mouth with the back of her hand.

—What's funny?

—There's the Evil Hungarian Consul.

—Why would he be evil?

—He offered to rent an apartment for me next door to the consulate so he could make love to me during coffee breaks. I asked if that was the condition for getting a visa to Hungary, and he said it was, but he gave it to me later anyway.

—Was it a nice apartment?

—Yes, very nice. It looks like a room at the Hermitage. But he wasn't—too old and disgusting.

—I see, being old is bad.

—Being disgusting is bad.

—And old is bad.

—It's bad but forgivable. You have no control of such things, but you can control yourself not to be disgusting. You aren't old.

—I will be in five years.

—Five years is a long time. We could be happy for five years. A five-year plan.

—And then what?

—Then we'd divorce. You wouldn't have to suffer the seven-year itch. You like this?

—Lovely. It's like a five-year economic plan?

—I'd give you the best years of my life. And you'll give me the mediocre years of yours. And maybe we'd stay married even after that. Maybe medical science will keep you alive till you are five hundred.

After I had been taking beta blockers for ten days, enough to be addicted, I researched the drug some more. Warnings about quitting beta blockers: extreme arrhythmia, sudden cardiac arrest, spiking blood pressure, plunging blood pressure, anxiety attacks. Shit, do I have to take this crap for the rest of my life? Oh, but maybe it's simply Pfizer propaganda? How can pianists take the drug before a performance and have no ill consequences? So if you take it occasionally and in moderation, you should be fine. However, one of the side effects is weight gain. And weight gain would increase my blood pressure and thus the need for beta blockers. Now, despite the relaxing properties of beta blockers, I was anxious, full of Angst and anguish and trepidation.

Yuliya and I drank in a wine bar near the Circus, on the north side of the Fontanka. This was not a tent but a solid red-brick building, a permanent circus. We went in and caught a show. Tigers were leaping through large burning rings. Then monkeys were supposed to ride white horses. Circus managers started whipping the horses and the monkeys. The monkeys freaked out and chased the managers and jumped into the stands and slapped the people and chased them. People shrieked and ran. The monkeys seemed to enjoy the mayhem and chased the customers. Luckily Yuliya and I were not in the front rows, but we also ran for the exit. It was a monkey revolution. The animals have had enough abuse. It accumulated from the Soviet era and they would not take it anymore. Twenty enraged chimps chased us all out.

—That was fantastic, a revolution. I said. What a horrible system to abuse all these animals for our fun.

—I will never visit a circus again.

—As long as you are in Russia, you are in a circus.

—Who was the ringleader, I said. —Did they have a Lenin there?

—To me, they all look like Lenin.

—Russia is such an energetic and unpredictable place, I said.

—So what? You have wife?

—No, I've been divorced for a few years.

—Why did you divorce? You were unfaithful?

—It's a long story, but in a nutshell, we lost the sex habit.

—How can you lose it?

—My wife couldn't conceive at first, and when she did, she dedicated herself to our kids. We had two sons, three years apart. She breastfed them, and she read that for babies, it's better to have creature comfort than to sleep alone, and she slept with the babies until they were three years old. So for six years I slept in my office. And my wife suspected that I must be sleeping around, and out of fear of cervical cancer, she didn't want to have unprotected sex. She'd read an article in the *New Yorker* about HPV causing cancer. She thought I gave her a urinary tract infection. I got tested, and I was clear, but she kept imagining. Of course, it stood to reason that I should have sex somewhere, and if not at home. . .but I was so obsessed with making money and work that I didn't seek it. And on the few occasions when we did have sex, it was like a medical exam. I should spare you the details. We just lost the intimacy. And when Rachel wanted to have sex again, I just didn't feel like doing it—found it too stressful to deal with her medical imagination and suspicions. And then she got a lover, which seemed fair, but there was no point in staying together.

I blushed and had another sip. Such a lame way to lose a marriage, to lose the Oedipal wars in the bedroom. Too simple even for psychoanalysis. And why the hell didn't we go into counseling? Because I didn't believe in psychology. I sighed, cleared my throat, and said, —This wine is getting to my head, I am all red.

—Do you pay child support?

—Of course.

—So you are a good man. A Russian man wouldn't bother to pay child support. Let's have a child and when we divorce, pay me three thousand dollars a month alimony. I think I could live on that.

—Why do you say that?

—And what are you doing with a young woman?

—We'll find out.

—You won't marry. You only want to have fun which you didn't in your marriage. What if I fall in love? *Stradayet Yulichka?* (Little Julia will suffer.)

—Does that happen, Ukrainians in love?

—It could happen. And then what? You travel back to America to your family and forget about Yulichka.

Tipsy, we walked out. I put my arm around her waist and we walked in parallel, our hipbones bopping in the rhythm of the walk.

—You have a fine body, I said.

—That I have.

—Why are you so confident about it?

—I was a gymnast for ten years, and I trained six hours a day. I was second in Ukraine in a junior championship and tenth in the world.

—Why didn't you continue?

—My older friends who kept at it ended up with all sorts of injuries, busted knees, hips. One of them is in a wheelchair. All that jumping and twisting is good for a child and terrible for an adult.

—The benefits are quite visible on your body.

—If I had continued with gymnastics, do you think I'd have any curves?

When we entered the yard, at dusk, the homeless crew was cackling and laughing. One bum was trying on a pair of shoes, which seemed a little too large, and he adjusted that by putting folded newspapers at the heel.

—They are funny, aren't they? I said.

—I am not looking at them. When you are a girl, you never look at the clochards.

Upstairs in my wobbly apartment, I opened a bottle of red wine (there was one 24-hour store that sold me contraband Moldovan wine), and we drank and kissed.

—Now we are married, she said.

—In that case, let's undress.

—You want to?

—Yes, it would be nice.

—OK, go ahead.

I stood up and with shaking hands unbuckled and pulled down my pants and my Hanes underwear.

—Nice, Yuliya said. You look healthy.

—What do you mean, healthy? Touch it then.

Yuliya leaned back in her armchair and kept her hands together as though in prayer. —Not right now.

—OK, your turn.

—No, I am fine this way.

—But we agreed, we'd undress.

—I didn't say I would. I said, You go ahead. Besides, it's kind of chilly tonight. Can you close the window?

—And then you'll undress?

—I am not that kind of girl.

—What kind are you?

—The marrying kind.

—You are a twenty-eight-year-old virgin?

—I'll tell you what you need to know.

—Fine, have another glass.

We finished the bottle and went to the window over the creaky floor, china clanking in the cupboard.

—I better go home, she said.

—Why, you are too drunk to go home now.

—You can accompany me.

We embraced and kissed. Now we were both topless, and I enjoyed the cool sensation of her skin against mine. We kept touching and undressed further.

—You like touching.

—Yes, it's great, I said.

—Don't you want to do anything else?

—You would have sex before marriage?

—To see what it would be like.

—So, like an engagement proposition?

—Yes, making love should be a proposition, for doing things together. Making marriage.

Suddenly I panicked. What if all those beta blockers combined with the alcohol and Zocor blocked me from getting an erection? Maybe I should have got another pill to make sure I'd be ready, but I had not imagined I'd have an opportunity to make love.

—Well, let's work at it. You know, after all that wine, I might need some stimulation. Just play with it for a while.

—You mean, like in a porn movie?

—You've seen one?

—Of course, Silly.

—Maybe you've even made one?

—That is crazy. What do you think of me?

—You are a very fine girl.

—Prove it.

—You should prove that you are a very fine girl.

—By following a porn script?

—No, of course not.

—Then what script?

—This is unscripted.

—You are right.

Mosquitoes buzzed all around us and the buzz lulled me and I fell asleep.

When I woke up, with the cool breeze of the dawn blowing in, I saw her curled up in the armchair by herself.

My throat was dry and sore, and I got up to drink water straight from the tap. I had no water in the refrigerator, and it wouldn't be the first time; so what if I got giardia or a bit of mercury or radiation. Wouldn't I get such creatures and elements and phenomena in the States, even from a healthy meal, such as a salmon salad? And maybe I wasn't getting any radiation. And what difference did it make? I had fallen asleep with a sex bomb, and nothing went off.

—*A hrapyet tebya hvatayet?* she asked. But snore you can very well.

—I made a mistake and took a beta blocker with too much wine.

—Do Americans take a lot of drugs?

—Oh, come here, let's cuddle.

—*Zelanya nyet.* I don't feel like it.

At five, when the subways opened, I accompanied her to the Gostiny Dvor subway entrance. We hugged like American acquaintances, without much longing, in lieu of a handshake or kiss, the kind of hug one could give an in-law after a funeral.

As I watched her descend into the deepest subway in the world, I thought I better get off those meds, and relearn how to live and love. Maybe writing a story would tranquilize me.

CHAPTER NINE

I struggle to maintain my personal space

IN KOFYE HAUZ, staying awake on several cups of double cappuccinos, I typed next to the thick wall and recounted how Milošević had his employer, Stambolić, assassinated, and how, in prison, he persuaded his doctor to give him all sorts of stimulants, including sex performance enhancers. And in my story, he dies of an overdose of Viagra during his wife's visit to his prison. I had no proof for that theory, so the story would be fiction. Maybe I could set another story in a Russian prison, perhaps about Dostoevsky? But then, there were probably way too many novels featuring Dostoevsky. *Master of St. Petersburg* by Coetzee, for example. I had been to Petropavlovsk, where Dostoevsky had been detained (on the orders of a Vladimir Nabokov ancestor—V. Nabokov's rabid dislike of Dostoevsky's work perhaps stemmed from an old family feud), but as it was merely a museum, Petropavlovsk gave me no real feel for what it was like to be in a Russian prison, but Kresty would.

After struggling with the story, I walked to the beer garden in front of the Kazan cathedral, at eleven in the evening, while red sunrays were reflecting off the golden cross. In front of a white and pink ice cream parlor—a troika coach—I ordered a half-liter can of *Pshenichnaya*, and drank thirstily. I could see the foamy lines—each an inch apart from the next—that marked the level of beer between my gulps. One problem with all that beer was that I had the urge to take a leak, and I looked longingly towards dark spaces near the cathedral. The sooty massive edifice, chipped in many places, looked *uzhasna*, horrifying. Stalin had transformed the cathedral into a museum of superstition and atheism. Through the cracks below the cathedral a dozen of cats' eyes fluoresced. Two policemen—dressed in military fatigues, with billy clubs and Kalashnikovs, in Adidas sneakers—walked by me noiselessly.

My friends, Sam and Mario, joined me, and several of their acquaintances from Columbia sat with us. Mario knew lots of Soviet jokes, and there was no stopping him from telling this one: *Brezhnev is opening the Olympic Games in Moscow. He reads the prepared text. Oh! The crowd shrieks, and when they quiet down, Brezhnev continues the speech. Oh! The crowd claps loudly, but a bit hesitantly. Brezhnev quiets them with a gesture. The crowd is quiet. The speechwriter leans over and says Comrade Presidyent, the text is a little lower, no need to read the top of the page.*

One person at the table said, —I don't get it.

—Brezhnev was reading the Olympic emblem.

—Who says that it doesn't get dark during White Nights? I said.

—But not that dark, Sam said, and pulled at his beard. Why don't they call them Gray Nights or Shadowy Nights?

—Shadowy would mean it was dark, I said. You don't get shadows in real darkness. Shadows would mean there was light.

—White Nights sounds better.

—Until recently, I thought they meant winter nights, when snow covered the streets, so . . .

—You have a point; because of the snow, winter nights aren't completely black either. You will see that St. Petersburg is all about pastel shades—no contrasts between the light and the dark.

—Sometimes I like darkness, I said. It has its uses.

I walked to the side of the cathedral between two rows of columns set so close together that it was indeed dark there. I looked around, and saw nobody, and so I pissed with a pleased sigh, and watched the urine darken even further the sooty columns. A large tomcat meowed at me.

As I was following the wise principle, shake well after use, an obnoxious spotlight hit me, blinding me momentarily. What is that? It sure can't be a religious moment, like Saul being converted on the way to Damascus by suddenly being struck blind with light from heaven. This light comes from the side, from below.

—What do you think you are doing! a gravelly voice shouted.

—Sorry. I didn't know where to go.

—What do you mean you didn't know? Go back to your hotel. And don't you see these public toilets?

—But the lines are too long and they are disgusting.

—What you are doing is more disgusting. Where are you staying?

The policemen were shining brazenly at my fly as I was buttoning it up—three of them. I could count silhouettes, but I could not see their faces.

—Papers, please, one of them said.

I showed them my driver's license from New York.

—Your passport?

—I left it in my apartment. I don't want the passport to be stolen. Here's a photocopy, though.

—No papers?

—The photocopy is a paper.

—The Russian law insists that you have the original on you at all times while in Russia.

—Really, is that the law? Even in a banya? I don't see how you could take a hot bath and still have a passport on you.

—In a banya you could urinate all you want and nobody would see it. Come with us!

They grabbed me above my elbow and dragged me into a Moskvich parked behind the Kazan in front of the *Lyod* Bar (ice bar). The bar was done all in blue, and everything there, including the glasses, was made out of ice. They drove a few bumpy blocks and took me to a police station. Even the stairs had a urine smell to them. Either a drunk policeman could not contain himself, or somebody performed an act of courage and civil disobedience right where it's most dangerous to do it.

Pretty soon I was seated in front of a yellow table. A thin, bony-faced police inspector with a gray crew cut faced me. He smoked cigarettes as nearly everybody who had a job and everybody who didn't have a job in Russia seemed to do. No wonder these men had a lowered life expectancy—during Yeltsin, as low as fifty-seven years and now close to sixty. It's attributed to excessive drinking, but though less spectacular, the excessive smoking seemed even nastier. And true enough, the inspector stuck out his tongue, which was probably stung by tobacco, and he smacked his lips, his face contorting into an expression of disgust. I was not sure whether the disgust had to do with me or with the taste of cigarettes, but it did have a depressive psychological effect.

The inspector kept smoking and scrutinizing me without a word until he finished the cigarette. He crushed the cigarette under his thumb in an aluminum ashtray. —So, you come from America, he said in English.

—Right.

—I didn't ask you. So, you come from America to piss on our sacred sites.

—I wasn't allowed into a bar—they asked for a big cover. And it was a strip club; aggressive topless women waving me in. I am sure I would have to give them quite a bit of money or they wouldn't leave me alone. All the restaurants have guards in front of them.

—They would let you in. Are you scared of women? They like foreigners. And there's Kofye Hauz.

—It's two blocks away.

—So? You can walk. Americans can walk. Sometimes people say Americans cannot walk, but I have seen them walking.

—True, that would have been the best.

—You could piss in the canal, or in the park, anywhere but on the holiest cathedral in all of Russia! If you go to Rome, do you piss on St. Peter's Cathedral? What kind of conduct is this?

—I am sorry. It was the darkest place I could find. Plus, I didn't know it worked as a cathedral; all I knew was that it was a museum of atheism.

—Fifty years ago it was. Our holy men are called to God there now. What you have done is terrible insult. You know, urinating in public alone is punishable, but what you did is worse than burning American flag in Washington.

—For heaven's sake! I didn't pay attention, I just needed relief, there was nothing deliberate in this.

—No attention. You did not notice the cathedral?

He smoked another cigarette and didn't say a word while it lasted. He crushed the butt in the tray and stared at me with his eyebrows raised. I sneezed.

—You have cold?

—I don't think so.

—Maybe you have allergies? Americans have allergies.

—No.

I sneezed again.

—Sensitive nose. Now, we must punish you.

—Because I am sneezing?

—Not just sneezing—many things together, American syndrome. I think we'll put you in jail.

—Could I give you the cash I have, fifty dollars, and you could let me go? I am sure that is more than you charge Russian citizens for such a minor offense.

—Did I hear you? You want to bribe authority? That is illegal. Your fine will have to be higher now because you tried bribe.

—I didn't try to bribe you. I just suggested maybe you have some kind of fine I could pay and you could let me go.

—You don't have passport. You haven't registered your stay with police.

—I did register a while back, I just don't have a photocopy of the registration on me. And the passport is in my apartment.

—You don't have registration on you. This is illegal. And why are you in Russia?

—This is a fascinating country, and I want to write about it.

—What have you written? I shall google. He turned to the computer, which cast blue light over his face, making him look even paler and grayer.

—The book is not out yet. I am a historian. History takes time. Maybe I will write fiction too.

—So you are not writer. I should type report: sacrilege, insult to the state, improper exposure in public place, urinating in public place, lack of proper documentation, insubordination to police, attempt to bribe, nose problems . . . you know, you might be tried for each of these offenses separately.

—Sneezing is not a crime.

—I am not asking your opinion. I am informing you. And I am not talking about sneezing.

—Could I make a phone call to a friend? Or to the American consul?

—I don't see point.

—They should know what's happening with me.

—If he's worried, he can call police.

—He knows many important people here.

—So do I.

—Could I pay a fine and go? You know, in America, you can at least deposit a bail.

—Yes, I am familiar with this system. It favors rich men. We aren't so corrupt here.

—I read that the whole country is run by the mafia, and everybody pays up to run any kind of business.

—How about America? Do you think we don't know that Skull and Bones runs the country? Tell us about mafia! Our mafia is amateurs, but yours runs the world. You think you are better than everybody else, you can piss on us.

—It just looked like that, but it was not a statement. I did it in the dark, hoping nobody would see me. A statement is something out in the open.

—How do I know you are not member of Skull and Bones? Did you study at Yale?

—It just so happens that I did, but only as a graduate student. That's a club for undergraduates. I knew where it was but never went in.

—You want me to believe that. You didn't go in and have sex with George Bush and John Kerry?

—If I had more influence, you think I would be here?

—We are used to American spies. Undress.

—What?

—Undress.

—Why?

—To see whether you are hiding anything.

—Are you serious?

—When wasn't I serious? You think Russians have sense of humor?

—I've just heard a good Russian joke. Would you like to hear it?

—I know, the whole country is a joke, but that's beside the point. When you undress, you want to be charming?

—I don't want to undress. That's certainly not the protocol.

—Tell me about protocol. It's not protocol to urinate on Holy Cathedral.

—Well, Stalin turned some churches into public urinals. He turned the Temple of Christ the Savior in Moscow into a swimming pool and a massive urinal.

—You are not Stalin. And this is not a communist country. Undress, *pozhalusta*.

—I won't.

—So, it's true. Insubordination. I was not sure about that charge, but thank you, you confirmed it. That will be additional punishment.

—I don't see how it would change anything.

—You make transgression, you must be searched, and we do body search.

—That's strange.

—You could do it easily or we could make you. Let's not waste time.

—Do you have a Miranda law in this country?

—Miranda is not a common name in Russia. We have no Olga and Tanya laws for that matter. Never heard of Miranda.

—You don't understand. I should have the right to remain silent.

—But you keep sneezing. We should check.

—I sneeze through my nose.

—You think I don't know this?

—You want to see whether I am dressed warmly enough, or something, to see why I sneeze? That doesn't make sense.

—It will all make sense, you will see.

The inspector smoked another cigarette. I couldn't imagine why it would be necessary to undress unless it was a form of humiliation. The policeman crushed the cigarette with his yellow finger.

—Don't make us use strong measures.

Oh, the hell with it, I thought. I stood up and with a trembling hand undid my belt and buttons. My jeans had the old-fashioned buttons, rather than a zipper.

The inspector stared calmly, and then stood up. He walked around the table and scrutinized the pants.

—Ah, Calvin Klein underwear? Take it off. Now, why do you need designer underwear? Skull and Bone people wear Calvin Klein underwear? George Bush?

—He would be more likely to wear Ralph Lauren Polo.

—I was right. You would know.

I dropped the underwear on the floor and it stayed there, encircling my ankles.

—Step out of it.

I did.

—Not bad, said the inspector.

—He took it up between his thumb and forefinger, and carried it to his desk, and then dropped it in his business case. Then he rang the bell on his desk.

A uniformed policeman walked in.

—*Gospodin* David Mariner, bend forward, the inspector said.

—Why?

—Don't interfere with process. Maybe you have drugs above your prostate.

—I don't.

—How do I know? Now, I don't like doing this, so my assistant will check cocaine.

—But that's insulting. I have never even tried any.

—Like Bill Clinton, do not inhale? You put it in nose and didn't snort? We have seen enough of your kind. They fly into Russia with cocaine in their anuses. Especially you Americans, you can't live without drugs. Many Americans come here to eat painkillers. Pharmacies ran out of codeine several years ago because American tourists ate it all. Now you need prescription to get it, all your fault. What's so good about painkilling? Pain is good, builds character.

—I agree with you. I don't understand why people like painkillers. When I had a car accident and took them, they dried up my mouth, made my heart palpitate, but the pain was still there.

—You don't have cold or allergies. Why are you sneezing? There is no other explanation.

—But that's outrageous. I demand that you give me a phone so I can call an end to this.

—You can make many phone calls when you leave jail. Maybe week, maybe month, maybe year? Nobody knows.

—This is criminal! I am going to write about this to the embassy, to the newspapers, you will pay for this!

—Criminal? You are criminal.

The young policeman with slick black hair and rotund cheeks, his dark eyes shining gleefully, approached me, putting a kid glove on his fist.

—It's not so bad. Your doctors do it. How old are you?

—Forty-eight.

—Forty-eight? I thought you were thirty-three. You Americans don't drink, don't smoke, and use Nivea every night? That's why you look so soft and young for a long time? At your age, doctors stick their fingers up your anus. What's problem?

—It's humiliating.

—And at forty-eight piss on holy cathedral not humility. How do you think the Holy Mother of Kazan felt?

—She felt nothing. She died a long time ago.

—Her icon is there, on that side of the Cathedral where you . . . you. . .

The cop sighed and lit up another cigarette.

The young policeman performed the examination. I ground my teeth. At one point, though it did not hurt badly—it did hurt a little—I felt tears coming to my nose, and that humiliated me even more. That I should admit that they were humiliating me and inflicting pain . . . that is indeed humiliating and painful.

—What are the results? asked the inspector.

—Negative. Nothing there.

—No drug sack?

—*Nichevo.*

—And what's his prostate like? Swollen?

—*Ne znayu.*

—Do it again, then. Slowly, and move the tip of your finger left and right, forward and back, with more feeling.

—But this is . . . I am going to call the ministry! I said.

—The ministry of what? Cultural Ministry? You may call Cultural Ministry when you buy art and want to export it. A few of my friends are artists. When you get out of prison, I help you buy art at good price.

—Ministry of Health. You are not qualified to do medical examinations. I looked at him suspiciously, in my bent position, under my armpit. —You will help me buy art?

—You think I know nothing about art and health. You are arrogant. And how do you know I didn't study medicine? I did, and that's where I met my wife, and she is a doctor. —Keep fingering, he addressed his underling.

The inspector inhaled deep and let two streams of smoke come out of his nostrils. The examination went on silently.

—Not even a swollen prostate. Seems normal, said the young policeman.

—And your glove is clean now? Nothing dirty? Maybe he washes up with a water bottle? Is he circumcised?

—What, now we are getting into religion? I said.

—That's where we started, my friend. How can you object to religion? I didn't think you had any respect. If you want to keep religion out of your penis and ass, you should keep your penis and ass out of religion. I recommend that, for the future, keep it all out.

—He is circumcised.

—My parents weren't religious.

—Circumcised and totally clean anus.

—All I can eat here is meat, so my ass is clean by default as I am constipated, that would be my guess.

—Catholics use toilet paper, which doesn't work too well, said the inspector.

—What nonsense is that?

—Congratulations, said the inspector, after taking a swig from a bottle of water. You are healthy. But you know what that means? You should be able to hold your urine better. If your prostate swollen, we would understand you must make urine, but with normal prostate, no excuse.

—Was that the purpose of this exam?

—We are precise.

—How about beer? Beer is hard to contain.

—If you can't hold it, drink vodka.

—But you sell it to tourists, what do you expect them to do?

—We expect them to urinate. By the way, I don't sell beer.

—It's a trap then. You make sure they can't go anywhere, and when they can't contain themselves, you imprison them!

—What do you do in America?

—Hard to explain.

—You criminal? And you said journalist?

—Not journalist.

—The two would be good combination. Do crime research then write crime in jail.

—I used to work as an investment banker but now I am one of those guys who help with online investing. When something goes wrong for an online investor, he can call in, and I can explain to him what is going on, and if his order didn't fill, I can track it down, making sure that his order went correctly as a market order, or a short, or a put, oh, I don't want to get technical with you.

—So, not writer. You liar.

—I am changing my career. Maybe historian. Maybe wine importer.

—I read about that. In America, you have many careers, ten years one career, ten years another, until you turn ninety. True?

—I hope so. I do the online stuff during the day and then at night, when I have the energy, I try to read and write.

—You try to read. Is it hard to read? Well, what is your salary?

—None of your business.

—Is it twenty thousand dollars a month?

—More like eight thousand, take home.

—Take home?

The inspector looked delighted, and smiled, revealing teeth in different shades and colors, white, yellow, gray.

—You want me to take home eight thousand. You have it right here? It's not up in your anus, so where?

—No, take home—that means, after taxes.

—You pay taxes? You must? Become Russian citizen, and you don't pay taxes. Depardieu will be new Russian.

—Is that easy to do?

—Do you have rich relatives? What are you worth to them? They could pay at least thirty thousand dollars. That is rational price for freedom.

—You couldn't get away with kidnapping Americans. George Bush is about to visit the city, and . . . you know, I can't just disappear.

The strange tobacco smoke, which seemed to contain cinnamon, kept stinging my eyes and making me sneeze, so that tears came to my eyes and glazed the scene. The yellow of the table broke into golden shafts of light.

—Don't you think that giving us thirty thousand dollars would be good practice of justice? What did you do to be rich? We work hard and we live with two hundred dollars in month, your cars burn our oil, and you think this is justice? What kind of car do you drive?

—I used to have a Jeep Cherokee, but now that I am single again it's a Celica.

—I knew it. Cheap Shirokee.

—I agree your salaries should be bigger. You do such good work. (I am not sure he noticed my irony.)

—So . . . it's not bad idea then, you agree?

—Basically, I am broke.

—We found out you are healthy. You are not broken. You realize we could shoot you and dump you in the Finski Zaliv and nobody will know who did it. Then you are broken. It will look like accident. Drunk tourists die. One more or less, what is difference? We could have a Cheap Shirokee drive over your body.

—Are you threatening me?

—You not smart. That's why they fired you as banker and you will never be good writer. Americans can't write good, not like we can, like Dostoevsky or Tolstoy. You have anybody like Tolstoy?

—Do you have anybody like Tolstoy or Dostoevsky in current Russia? Russians can't write any longer either. Anyway, what does Dostoevsky have to do with you?

—How do you know I am not writer. Russians very talented people.

—Writing makes one gentle and compassionate, and you seem, if you don't mind my saying so, a bit cruel. By the way, it's funny that you, like many Russians, keep skipping the articles a and the.

—Cruel? Talking to you gentle, not fracturing skull.

The inspector—after yawning—addressed the young policeman in Russian, —Put him in the cell, see what he thinks later, when he is sober.

There were brown stains on the mattress. I didn't know whether those came from blood. There were brown stains on the wall. And strangely enough, even the cell smelled of urine. There was a stand-up toilet at one end of the room, with a small tank of water atop it to flush down the waste. The handle on it was broken, however.

I put my pants back on. It was strange not to have any underwear. What if they came in and beat the hell out of me and bloodied me? Who knows, they might do that, just for fun. And to think of it, being a cop was a wanted job. In Moscow, people bribed up to $30,000 to get the position which paid, officially, $200 a month. It's clear how the cops improved their income. In a way, Russia was an unbeatably rational country: if you want to be a criminal, what better job to have than a policeman's?

CHAPTER TEN

Thanks a million!

An hour later, the door clicked and the assistant led me to the chief's office.

The chief exclaimed happily, —Oh, nice to see you, my friend. Have a nice day!

—What do you mean?

—I am practicing phrases you Americans like. You know, my job is pretty boring, so at least I can pick up a few languages. Thanks a million!

I wondered what occasioned the mood swing, and then noticed a bottle of Johnny Walker gripped by his left hand.

—You are lucky, my friend. I decided: too much work to seek ransom from your family. And no point in keeping you in jail for month. We need space for many other tourists. This right here is great real estate, each hour in this room could be worth two hundred dollars, so we won't keep you. It doesn't pay.

—Oh, thank you.

—Say, thanks a million.

—OK, thank you very much.

—Why say very much, when million is more precise? That doesn't mean that we let you go now. I decided you must pay penalty, five hundred. And then I can say, Thanks a five hundred.

—But I don't have it on me.

—Don't complain or you must pay more. Five hundred includes prostate examination. When did you have prostate examination last?

—My doctor doesn't like doing it. He says when I am fifty, he'll do it.

—See? You think we like? That's dirty work—worth two hundred dollars in America. You get it cheap here. I know you have only fifty dollars in your body. But you have credit card. We shall use it.

They led me into a black Lada and drove through strange-looking dilapidated streets behind Gostiny *dvor*, the old shopping mall which occupied a whole city block, and they avoided the streets which were torn up for new sewage and water systems. We seemed to be going in circles before we emerged onto Nevsky in front of the Nevsky Palace hotel. We walked past the guards and porters to the cash machine. I put in the card and typed my pin code and took out five hundred dollars. The inspector took the money and put it inside his jacket, right above his pistol, strapped on the side.

—Thanks a million! Oh, thanks a five hundred. Have a nice day, Mr. Mariner. Would you like a ride back to your hotel? May I help you?

I'd have preferred to be rid of their company right away, even if it meant walking a mile, but as I hesitated, the inspector said, —Normally we'll give you a ride. We don't want you to get into trouble.

Near the exit stood two tall blondes in fox fur coats. They both wore vermilion lipstick. One of them, though dishrag blonde, looked familiar. Was it Masha? She may have dyed her hair.

The inspector grinned, revealing a silver molar, when he noticed that I was staring.

—Would you like some pleasure, Mr. Mariner? Maybe if they examine your prostate, not feel so bad.

I didn't reply, and the inspector was already chatting with the ladies, in Russian. —We have got you a bargain, he said to me. One hundred fifty dollars till dawn.

What does dawn mean here? It is already dawn, it's White Nights, isn't it? You mean five minutes?

—They are so hot, I bet you not last longer.

—Masha, is that you?

—Why would I be me? she replied.

It was Masha, no doubt. Just one sentence, and something screwy is going on.

—Good new hairdo. By the way, can you return my five thousand rubles? I could use the money.

—For what? To sleep with me? What do you think of me? Maybe you could afford my friend with that, but not me.

—No, to pay the fine to the police.

—I warned you about them. If you listen, you save money.

—That's true.

—So, I don't owe you. I would have saved you more than three thousand. I am sure they got fifteen out of you.

—About that. How did you know?

—I know how they work. Petrushka always aims for that much.

—Petrushka? The ballet?

—No, I call him that. Pyotr.

The inspectors said, —You know the ladies? You ask them for sex? It is illegal like in America. You should pay fine for this.

—Oh, come on, I asked her for nothing, just for money.

—You asking her for money?

—She owes me one hundred and ten dollars.

—My God, you are so petty! Masha exclaimed. —Why ten dollars?

—Let me understand, the inspector said. —This hooker owes you money?

—Why do you think she is a hooker?

—Therefore, you are her boss? Pravda? You pimp?

—No, I am not a pimp, that's crazy.

—If you want to work in our district, you must pay for permission, two thousand dollars a month.

—I am not a pimp!

—That is only one hundred per day. Cheap. *Dyeshevo.*

—But *dyevushek nyet dyesheve.*

—See how money goes here? Masha said. —You were surprised I need money. Everybody needs it and nothing else. Look at these cops.

—Sometimes men want sex.

—Nobody in Russia wants sex. I think you could have observed this. We have other problems.

—So, Gospodin Mariner, will you pay for your permit? the policeman who was checking messages on his cellphone asked.

—What kind of permit?

—Pimp protection.

—Pimps don't piss in the streets, they have titty bars where they can do that.

—Haven't thought about this. Maybe you not pimp? The inspector looked at me, blasting smoke out of his nostrils. —Then you may want sex from ladies?

—No, thank you.

—Two hundred dollars discount rate.

—But you said one hundred before.

—That was joke. Fine ladies here. It is three hundred. One hundred for lady, one for pimp, one for hotel.

—Who is the pimp then?

—But we are friends, so you get discount. And it's very safe while I protect. And no pimp fee as they need no protection.

—I don't have any money.

—We go back to your machine. Only hundred dollars for room and room service.

—No, no. Thanks a million, I said.

—Good, my friend. Now you even have humor. Good man.

—The ladies are gone anyway. Where are they?

—You right about that. I think they are tired of cheap Americans. Brits and Russians not worry about money, and Americans argue like they buy real estate. Yes, they gone. Now you know how to walk home? You don't? No problem. We'll get you taxi.

—I can do that. It's easy to hail them down.

—But you are out and have no money. It's against law in America to walk without money, no? Littering?

—Loitering. It's not against the law in Russia, is it?

—No, not for Russians, but maybe for Americans.

—It's illegal for foreigners to be here without money, the assistant said. —We could arrest you for that too, *znayete*?

—That is absurd. I have no money because you took it.

—And you call dollars money?

Despite being worried, I laughed. —That reminds me of an anecdote. Orthodox Jews are not allowed to carry money on Sabbath, but in Poland, they made an exception for Zlotys, claiming that was only paper, and the Talmud said nothing about carrying paper on Sabbath. At this rate, the Orthodox will soon be allowed to carry hundred-dollar bills on Sabbath!

—You think you can be charming and tell jokes and not pay fine?

—But you just made up the law, you are joking!

—We didn't make up law. America did. Don't you want to be treated American?

The cops tapped me on the shoulder, once on the left, once on the right. —We'll give you a ride, to protect you from other police. The police could arrest you for littering.

—I am not loitering.

—And to make sure you don't just piss in the streets. Must you? Pissing may count. To be safe, we take you.

—*Ne nado.* I have a one hundred note on me.

—I don't believe you, said the chief. Where?

—Here, in my jeans' watch pocket. I pulled out a folded and crumpled red hundred-ruble note.

—You hid it from us.

—No, you never asked for it.

—And is that the way to treat Russian money? You just fold it like that, and crumple it, and roll it into a ball, until it's junk?

—It's folded neatly.

—It will break at the crease like that. It's against law to tear up rubbles. Rubbles are protected. But we are nice, we forgive. Come, we give you ride.

From not sleeping, with the drink wearing off, I was dizzy. I ended up in the passenger seat. The young policeman drove and the inspector sat in the back next to a couple of submachine guns.

As the cab made a U-turn, I noticed two other policemen leading the two ladies into a black Mercedes. I wondered what the women would have to do now. Were they friends? Pale sunshine hit the gilded cross on the Kazan cathedral, which shone fiercely as though it had accumulated more gold during the night. The sunrays bouncing off the cross hurt my eyes, like needles treading through my retina, ultra-thin cosmic radiation-enriched rays poking my brain like an obstetrician's needle meshing an embryo.

—This is close enough, I said. —Here, in front of Dom Knygi would be good.

—We take you home, to your door. You can't walk, you are still drunk. And who knows where you urinate. Just don't look at cathedral.

—I am not.

They drove me around Bolshaya Konyushennaya, past the Lutheran church onto the one-way north Embankment of Griboedova.

—This is my building. You can let me off here. *Spasibo!*

—*Nichevo.* We'll drive you into the yard.

They drove into the yard, past the marriage agency. *Agenstvo Znakomstva.*

—Gospodin David perhaps wants one bride?

—No, I don't want any brides.

—You want young, maybe twenty-two? I have a niece like that.

—You are serious?

—When wasn't I serious? You are nice man from Yale. That would be good marriage for one niece. Nice for niece. You want her phone number?

—What would I say anyway?

—Uncle Pyotr told me to call you. Simple. We could be family! What would you call that in English?

—I'd be nephew-in-law. But in America, that's distant family; nobody uses that term.

They drove to my *podyezd*, entrance. I stepped out and slammed the door.

—Not so strong! said the inspector. —You want to show us your apartment?

—I have to sleep now.

I fumbled for the keys and pulled them out, but the magnetic core had fallen out. Now I fingered my pocket depths among coins looking for the little magnet.

—Something smells like burning, the inspector said.

I inserted the magnet core into my key, matched the round magnet with the door keypad, and the heavy metal door clicked open. The black tomcat fluoresced from the second stair, and I was about to sail across the threshold, when the cop reiterated,

—Something is burning.

—That's normal around here.

The cops walked across the yard, through the children's playground with yellow and red swing sets, and through a large sandbox with sandcastles. I wanted to go up to my apartment but it wasn't clear to me whether I was allowed to—on the other hand, I wasn't under arrest, was I?

The Dostoevsky lookalikes were having a trash burning party which went out of hand. One garbage container was flaming up.

—Who started this fire? the cops asked one bum.

The inspector picked up my cell phone and called for a firetruck. I was surprised because that seemed to be the most obvious and rational reaction, and I came to expect no obvious and rational actions to be taken by the cops.

The bums walked away. I asked, —Why not interrogate them? You interrogated me.

—They are just bums, there's no point in bringing them to court or jail. No more point than taking a tree stump to court and blaming it for what happens in the yard.

—I understand. They have no money. You can't get any bail out of them.

—Usually they have no documents, no identity to demonstrate. It's hard to deal with them. It's strange you want us to arrest these poor people. What is burning in the garbage? Smells like meat.

—OK, I will marry your niece if you leave me alone.

—If you are innocent, you might qualify for family. Let's talk.

—Come back tomorrow after I've had some sleep.

—It's White Nights, nobody sleeps.

They drove me to the same interrogation station. —You wait here until we find out more about your yard.

They came back a few hours later. —We have found out quite a few things. There was a man in the garbage container, probably the man killed on Liteny several days ago. We have pictures of the car in hit-and-run, someone emailed those to us, and we didn't match the images before.

—Who?

—Not identified. But it seems you are the passenger there, and the man driving is a criminal we've been searching for a long time.

—You haven't been looking for him. He was a police chief, higher ranked than you.

—That doesn't mean he's not criminal.

—Touché.

—He's your partner?

—He was my cabbie. He picked me up as I was going to Kresty.

—Kresty? What for? You want to see it from the inside? We might help you.

—I've already seen it as a tourist.

—It's very simple. Give us twenty thousand, and you will not be suspect.

—But my credit card cash limit is only eleven thousand. My credit is not that good.

—As you wish. We'll let you sit in Kresty until you get more money, and if you don't, you know, we might convict you of murder and arson.

—Arson? That's crazy. I was here with you most of the night, you know that.

—We know that, but nobody else does. It's funny you are contesting arson and not murder. And we don't know—maybe those men in your yard work for you. Maybe you paid them to burn up the corpse.

—Rich fantasy.

—All that matters is not the facts, but what appears to be facts, and how we can present them.

—Unless I pay?

—First you run over a man in a car, and then he ends up in your garbage dump, out of all the dumps in the city. Coincidence? You and your partner drove the corpse here.

—I have no idea who dumped the body here. And why would it be the man from Liteny? And that was more than three weeks ago. How would the corpse show up only now? And how can you be sure it's that corpse? Maybe you put it here? I was at that time taking a tour at Kresty. You can go and see the records there. They record all the visitors.

—That will just prove that it was you on the way to Kresty. And you know who the pedestrian is?

—No idea.

—He was an importer of Georgian wines. And in your building lives another Georgian wine importer, right next door to you.

—So why not arrest him?

—Not a bad idea.

—He has money, I am sure.

—Good thinking, my friend. And we know one more thing. That there was another Georgian importer who was dumped in the same dumpster three weeks ago. We have witnesses.

—You mean, sex workers you can pay to say what you want them to say?

—A woman saw you with the corpse. She is not making it up.

—Why would you bring that all up right now and not before?

—Oh, before was just a little probe. Now we can be serious.

—So this was not just about pissing.

—We watched you, we have pictures from streets, bars, concerts. But don't worry about us. We don't have to tell you how our homeland security system works.

—Who has framed me? I can't believe this crap. You start out being thugs harassing people in the streets, and now you are the fucking Homeland Security!

—Watch your language. You think Russia needs no Homeland Security and America needs? Have you ever been to Georgia?

—No.

—But you know Georgians.

—Only a cleaning lady from Kofye Hauz.

—Yes, and she has invited you to Batumi.

—I'd never go there.

—It's nice there. And you eat at Georgian restaurants.

—Don't you? I can't eat plain Russian food, I need spice, garlic, peppers. All my Russian friends eat at Georgian restaurants. Is there such a thing as Russian food? Such a large country, so little imagination when it comes to cooking. Russia is as bad as Germany and England. These countries have no food of their own worth savoring, so they've gone around invading countries simply to get a taste of a decent meal. Without Georgia and Armenia, Russia would've had to invade China and India.

—I see why we couldn't find any cocaine on you. You swallowed it and now you are raving. You travel too much. Look at your passport. All these stamps. What kind of business are you?

—I told you everything about me.

—Why would you be killing wine importers? Competition?

—I am interested in drinking wine, but I don't work in the wine business.

—You are interested in Kresty? You are a journalist? Fine, we'll help you and take you there.

—You can take me there just like that?

—What did you think, that we are not real police?

—I was warned that most people who look like police in the street are not police, and the people who don't look like police are.

—Down the stairs we go.

A policeman opened the door of the black Lada.

—I am not coming along. I need a lawyer.

—There will be plenty of lawyers. In murder cases there usually are.

—This is insane! I'd never kill anybody. Innocent until proven otherwise.

—Wait for the cocaine to quit working, and you calm down. Here, you are guilty until you prove you are not guilty. Get a good alibi.

—I will, but if you are really taking me, let me first feed my poor cat.

—I like cats, said the inspector. I'll feed her some sardines.

CHAPTER ELEVEN

Doing time at Kresty

WHO FRAMED ME and why? In whose cobweb was I a fly?

I spent the first night in a solitary cell before I would be transferred to a communal one.

—You are lucky, said the supervisor, —this is one of our best cells. You have your own toilet. And tonight you can stay here for free. Otherwise, we charge for the superior accommodations.

—You charge for staying here?

—Yes. It used to be for free during Socialism but now we must run a good business and be solvent.

—Does it mean you arrest only people who have money?

—Tell me it's any different in the United States.

—That is crazy, to be paying to stay in jail. Can I pay to stay out of jail?

—You are trying to bribe me?

—I don't want to be paying to stay where I don't want to stay.

—Don't worry, we have rooms for free, where you stay with eight people, and then you'll beg to pay for this one. Tonight is on me, a little token of friendship.

The warden extended his hand, and it took me a couple of seconds to realize that a handshake was being offered. I grasped the hand, which was cool, long, and soft. The warden didn't squeeze but simply held out his cool hand as though it was not part of him, but a found object, a Halloween-style joke, an imitation of a severed arm. I pulled at it, sort of expecting it to fly out of the sleeve, but it stayed, apparently real.

—*Dobro pozhalovat!* the warden said. —You could call me Drug Popov. Let me know if you need anything.

—Is there a pillow here?

—You don't need a pillow. You could use your shoes and put your pants over them, and that will work.

—I'd prefer a pillow.

—That will be five hundred rubles.

—That's more than a new one costs.

—As you wish.

—I don't have the money on me.

—No problem. We can keep a tab going.

I followed the warden's advice and used my shoes for a pillow. The air was musty and too warm. I had no access to my pills, and I wasn't sure whether I was anxious because of that, or, naturally enough, because of being in a foreign prison of ill repute under serious charges. At the moment, not having any beta blockers and other drugs might be a bigger problem than prison. What if my blood pressure suddenly shot up and my heart went into shock? That would be a sorry end of a life. What would be left after me? I could have just as well not lived, which probably would have been better as it would have left no mess behind me. Maybe there would be an article about the Russian prison system—maybe even about me. There would be speculations, and they would amount to something grander and more adventurous than my life: an American mafioso, after killing two Georgian importers of wine and mineral water, is murdered at Kresty by Spanish mafia.

At two in the afternoon, the warden opened the door and said, —If you like, you can take a walk in the yard. You don't have to pay for it.

So on an unusually sunny day in that otherwise rainy July, I stood outside in the prison yard along the red-brick wall to catch some sunshine. Barbed wire sparkled in the sun. It seemed to be new, sharp, with a bunch of little blades. It wouldn't cross my mind to attempt to jump such a high wall, but the wires made a jeering statement, —Ha, I bet you'd like to jump over me! Just you try and I'll shred your ass.

And if I climbed the fence, how could I cross the borders? My name would be listed in the border patrol system. Was Russia all that organized? It paraded as a land of severity and organization, while it was perhaps merely cruel. Cruelty can be a disguise, a smokescreen, to hide the lack of discipline. Wasn't Soviet airspace supposed to be impervious and that German, Rust, flew his hobby plane from Hamburg and landed it straight in the middle of the Red Square? I daydreamed of the border crossing. Maybe they would let me pass. Usually, it would be some bleached middle-aged person, scrutinizing you for a second, or looking like she or he is scrutinizing you, but perhaps only acting, so that if you scrutinized her/him, you wouldn't get an idea that—ok, let's use the noncommittal plural—they were in fact daydreaming, or covertly listening to junky music over an iPod. Just as Petersburg was based on imitation, so was the Russian border police raised on imitating the East German border police, who had imitated their notion of what Soviet border police was although it never was that precise. The major task of the border police always remained the same: collecting bribes, fines, and contraband, anything of worth to supplement the low salary. So if that was the case, why wouldn't I just walk out of the prison? There were only two registered cases of escape from Kresty. And probably none of them took place by climbing over a barbed wall.

I turned my neck to avoid eye contact with the motley crew of my new peers and winced from a shot of pain. There were body builders with tattoos on their biceps, dried-up consumptive types with all sorts of creases either from TB or lung cancer, young men who kept hopping from one leg to another and laughing, a few fat guys, and lots of guys who looked like traditional hockey players with a few front teeth missing, and a few well-groomed men.

I was allocated to a room with three bunk beds (six cots) and eight prisoners. As a newcomer, I would probably have to sleep on the floor. It was a horrible paradox that in the country which had more space than any other on earth people would be jammed like this.

—Hey, you, if you want to sleep on a cot, you can, if you give me a hundred rubbles, said a bodybuilder with uneven teeth. It seemed he had two rows of teeth, like a shark, but not so well organized; his teeth overlapped and pushed each other out of the way.

—How would I have one hundred? They took my last banknote.

—They'll take you out to get cash.

—How about if I sign a promissory note?

—You get money tomorrow and tomorrow night you'll sleep well. For now, Citizen of the United States of America, enjoy the floor.

Luckily it was summer, so I didn't freeze on the cold floor, but my bones were sore. At night I woke up in a cold sweat. The room resounded with snores and gasps and creaks and whistles. My heart was alternately palpitating for a couple of minutes and then shivering. Am I fibrillating? Maybe I should call for a doctor? Do they even have one here? They have a morgue, and a distinguished one at that. Many famous people died here; even Joseph Brodsky had worked in the morgue.

Perhaps I would have worked myself into a nervous breakdown if I had believed my thoughts. Well, I'd had opportunities for a breakdown earlier. I wondered why it hadn't happened, whether having silly thoughts and occasionally serious thoughts kept me essentially impervious to major psychological trouble. Maybe you have to be deep to break down. I just need to keep thinking in my trivial way and that should calm me down, better than meditation. If I sat in the lotus position in the cell, the inmates would laugh at me. Maybe the Shark would kick me. Thinking silly doesn't require ostentatious body postures; slouching the way I did would do just fine. Of course, slouching must be bad for my heart as it decreases the open space in my ribcage and exerts pressure. Perhaps that's part of my anxiety, the actual pressure on the heart. I stood up and straightened. Maybe my heart has the same problem that I do, too little space, jammed with too many ugly prisoners in the cage, nasty stomach and liver and spleen and lungs, all no doubt suffering their various crimes such as inhaling polluted and radioactive air and drinking alcohol. I didn't believe I could fall asleep with all the snoring, but in the morning, I found it hard to wake up.

My cellmates ate breakfast porridge from one pot. Eating oatmeal with all these men, who kept dipping their spoons and licking them, was not appetizing. Since I was starving, I ate, despite my gag reflex, which reminded me of being at a dentist's and having my tooth imprints taken.

After breakfast, while I was still struggling not to vomit—because if I vomited, I figured I would be even hungrier and more miserable—there was another banging on the metal door.

—Shower time! a guard shouted, and all the inmates, other than me, jumped and rushed out of the doors.

—How about you? the guard said. —You want to stay dirty?

—I don't feel like it, not today, maybe tomorrow.

—There's no tomorrow. It's now or next week. Each week you get one shower, fifteen minutes max.

—Only fifteen minutes?

—Believe me, that will be plenty.

In the shower, twenty men stood naked while a blast of cold water splashed over them for several seconds. The blast got me only peripherally, making me wet. The blast stopped, and the men were soaping their bodies and pushing each other out of the way. They were passing three or four bars of soap from one hand to the next, but I could never lay my hands on it, and I didn't know whether I wanted it. Does soap indeed kill all the germs? Maybe it feeds some.

—Can I have some shampoo? I asked a guard.

—You don't need shampoo. Wash your hair with soap.

—Well, can I have a bar of soap?

—Ask the men who have it.

The variety of tattoos on the prisoners amazed me—monsters, swear words, prayers, lines from Pushkin, the Bible, lyrics by Zappa . . . images of snakes, soccer balls and players, emblems of different countries and cities, five- and six–limbed stars and swastikas with the hands bent in the clockwise and counterclockwise direction (if it's counterclockwise, I guess it's not a Nazi swastika but merely a Hindu swastika), lions, eagles, sharks, two-headed eagles, four-headed, and so on. It was a grand tradition of prison tattoos, and those who were there for an indeterminate amount of time, many of them, indulged in this form of branding and marking, and once they left, they would always belong to the same club. Without a single tattoo and without much chest hair, I felt naked among the men. Being unmarked was a statement too: I am a greenhorn. Although I detested the fashionable tattoos such as I could see in the city, especially on the lower East Side along with piercings and rings, now I wished I could buy a tattoo, and of course I could; the prison featured a tattoo shop. The managers of the prison were clearly proud of their tradition. Maybe there were even soccer matches between different prisons, and I could get on a team and shape up.

The guard splashed the rabble with cold water, in a powerful blast from a hose nearly as thick as a fire hose. The jet of cold water hit me in the chest. Another blast hit my head, and the soap went into my eyes. Knuckling made my eyes bite more; I couldn't properly see in front of me, but a huge figure, a sort of sumo wrestler, spoke:

—Who do I see? Is that possible, Mr. Canada Dry! The last time I saw you, we had a big storm, and now another one.

—Sergei? I thought you were the law, that you put people in jail.

—I will be out of here in no time. These dumb fucks know nothing.

—Why are you here?

—I pushed an Azeri guy's head against the wall, just so, for the hell of it, the guy wouldn't drink enough, and he seems to have died.

—What do you mean, seems to?

—I didn't hang around to see. I thought he got up with the help of his friends, but then, the cops told me he died.

—You killed the guy?

—Something must have been wrong with him not to be able to take a little knocking. I've knocked many heads, but never such a soft skull, what can I say. Not my fault.

—I don't get it, why would you bash his head?

—I don't get it either, but when you are drunk, you can get carried away. And you, Canada Dry, what brings you here?

—Just a mistake. I was riding in a car which ran over a Georgian, and the guy apparently died, and now they blame me.

—Amazing, my friend, you too? I am proud of you. I saw something in you, but I didn't know you had it in you, to knock off one of those.

—You're misunderstanding me here. I was not the driver but a passenger. I am not a racist.

—Come here, my boy! No need to explain.

I stood on the foamy cement, with my balls shriveled with Sergei, whose balls also shriveled either from the cold or from contraband steroids. Despite the shower, he smelled of garlic and nicotine.

—What room? he asked.

—Why do you ask?

—Maybe we can be roommates. You can teach me French, and time will pass.

—I have nothing to do with the French.

—Come on, don't be shy now. Friends should stick together.

—True, true, I said, without meaning it.

In fact, I meant the opposite because Sergei, who was still wet, retaining probably several liters of water in the elaborate system of his chest and other body hair, gave me another huge and sticky hug. I was glad the guy had body hair because it was better than naked skin.

—Friends do stick together, I said, in Russian, so at least there was the linguistic consolation, if not the reptilian. If Hindu metaphysics had any influence in this latitudinal approach to the polar circle, and people were reborn as punishment, Sergei would be a reincarnation of a diplodocus.

—I am sure that for a small fee we could arrange to be roommates, he said.

—A small fee, to whom?

—The fucking warden.

—Do you know the warden?

—Do I know Popov! He is a decent man. It's not his fault that we are here. You can get everything you want from him if you give him enough cash.

At this point in the conversation, since the air outside the shower room proper was warm, the four balls that belonged to us two unshriveled, hanging.

—I think that if you paid only a thousand rubles you could have me as a roommate.

I thought I would pay ten thousand rubles not to have Sergei as a roommate but didn't pronounce my thoughts. I scratched an itching spot on my hairy buttock.

—They haven't stolen your credit card? Sergei asked. They are very fair about that. They do want you to have access to cash. You can be a source of income for months. So, if you are shy, I will talk to him, and for a little fee. . . You realize, they could waterboard you and get the pin code out of you and max out the credit card? Hello, Mr. Canada!

—I have nothing to do with Canada. You are thinking of a friend of mine.

—My friend, it's a fantastic thing to see you here. Even if you are a Jew.

—So, Canada Dry, what are you so silent about? I'll protect you here. You will not be anyone's prison bitch.

—How do you know that term?

—Break it up, you two, said the warden, and rolled up his sleeve, revealing a tattoo, with chess pieces wearing the faces of Putin and Yeltsin as kings and Bush Junior and Milošević as queens.

—Break what? Sergei said. —Do you know who I am?

—It's not my job to know. The break's over, and you two should go back like everyone else.

For lunch, I had hot dogs, *sosiski,* in soggy buns. Why is spam the butt of so many jokes? Hot dogs should be the ultimate butt. I chewed and thought of Sergei. How come he spoke such good English? And was he indeed a prisoner or was he planted as a provocateur?

One thing that I missed in prison was music. I was trained to become a pianist and had nearly made it, having gone through the Juilliard pre-college training on the piano. Now I listened in my head to the Hungarian Rhapsody No. 2 by Liszt, the nostalgic virtuosity. I was embarrassed to have such an imposter of a composer rummaging through my head, when Brahms, who was not Hungarian, struck the Hungarian chord combinations so much more convincingly than Liszt did, but that was perhaps simply because Brahms was running away from Beethoven's domain, looking for new territories. He could not compose symphonies after listening to Beethoven's symphonies, and it took him years to eke one, and then three more. He burned twenty string quartets, because each time he finished one, he'd hear a Beethoven quartet and burn his. His Hungarian music is so delightful and unfettered, as if his soul had taken a voluntary exile into the land without Beethoven. Nobody was playing music for me at the prison, but the music grew louder and louder. It was peculiar that so much music would be in my head while around me the cacophony of banged doors and coughing was going on. If I were a composer, I wondered, would I be able to make something of all these sounds?

CHAPTER TWELVE

Another export-import opportunity for me

I WOKE UP with a hard-on. Not taking any drugs may be good. Two days without beta blockers, and I was back to my youthful self. While waking up, I thought I heard prisoners sighing, and it seemed several of them were slapping their monkeys.

I had slept in my clothes. I had no toothpaste, and my mouth was sticky. The door opened, and a guard in a shabby gray uniform with a poorly designed baseball cap said: —David? Come forward. Follow me, for an interview.

—What do you need to interview me about?

—Don't talk to me, but to the boss.

—Who is the boss?

We walked down the hall past dozens of metal doors with small windows, to the director's office. The guard knocked. The door opened and Drug Popov waved me in. He pulled out a bottle of Tsarskaya vodka from the chest of drawers in his writing desk. The yellow gold imitation label glittered on the bottle.

—How are you, Gospodin David?

—I am innocent.

—Nobody is innocent. What does innocent mean? Paying the bills is the closest to it we are capable of. If you have money, you are welcome here, and you can buy your innocence.

—You mean, if I didn't have money, you'd release me?

—I don't have the power to do that, but if you had no money, I wouldn't be interested in talking with you, and maybe you'd rot in prison for years and nobody would know you were here. Anyhow, how did you sleep last night?

—It was terrible. I couldn't even get a bed. There are nine of us and only six cots. Half of the people snore like they are dying. You should check them for sleep apnea.

—Snoring is not bad for you. All real men snore. You'll get used to it.

—But to the lack of beds, I won't.

—Many foreigners tend to be gay, and they like to sleep in small beds with men.

—Well, I don't.

—So, you like to sleep with them in large beds?

—No, how do you conclude that?

—You denied liking it in small beds. You like it in big beds? You are gay?

—No.

—Why didn't you say so? Speak more clearly then.

—Your logic is the same as this one. Answer yes or no. Have you stopped beating your kids yet? No matter how you answer it, it turns out you have been beating your children. See?

—Here, have a shot of vodka.

—In answer to your first question, I hate sleeping on the floor.

—You had no sex?

—Why would I?

—And other prisoners had no sex?

—None, from what I could tell, unless you count masturbation.

—It counts. They did a lot of it?

The warden looked at me gleefully, expectantly. He took off his warden cap and rubbed his shiny top; it reflected the overhead lightbulb, which nestled in a round milky-hazy ball. Perhaps to make up for the baldness, the warden let the hair on his temples grow over his ears, and sideburns covered thick swaths of his cheeks.

I checked my pants. I still had a hard-on, without any apparent stimulus. Was I a masochist now, and being interrogated gave me a thrill? It didn't make sense—the ward manager with his broken boxer nose and uneven hair distribution was not a pretty sight.

—But you could hear them wanking off?

—I don't know what I heard except a lot of snoring, wiggling, tossing and turning, and much of it was mine. You don't want prisoners to have sex, do you? You give them bromides, I imagine, just as they do in most prisons all over the world. It's safer that way, isn't it?

—No, we don't do that. That would be inhumane. We give them Cialis in kasha every morning.

—You must be joking! Isn't that very expensive?

—No, this is Chinese Cialis, it's very cheap, maybe five rubles a pill.

—But why would you do that?

—Just an experiment, to see whether it works. You can never trust the Chinese and Indian pharmacology.

—I've heard that many times.

—But then, the Chinese are such good workers, why wouldn't they make this work? Still it's good to test it.

—On prisoners?

—Of course, on prisoners. That's a traditional testing ground. It's more reliable than testing rats. You Americans draw all your conclusions from rat results. We are more precise.

—Why not on yourself?

—Me? I don't need it. And watch what you are saying. I could interpret this as an insult.

—I didn't mean it that way.

—I need to test it on others first. I wouldn't want to poison myself or any of my friends. We'll first see that it's safe and effective. Stand up please!

I stood up.

—Come closer. The warden touched my crotch and massaged it. I shrank back. —What are you doing?

—Why are you jumping away? Don't worry, I only wanted to see that you have a hard-on and you do. That is wonderful, my friend. Even Americans get erections. Chinese medicine is working!

—I don't want any more Cialis in my breakfast.

—A nice-looking man like you, it's good for you to have erections. Not having them may lead to heart failure.

—I have high blood pressure and Cialis could kill me. You know, like that African president who ordered six prostitutes to sleep with him and he took one Viagra pill per prostitute, six doses, all at once, and died.

—That will not happen to you. You will not get six prostitutes here. Anyway, we give you only one pill every day. And that is very generous of us. Find another prison that does it!

—I am not prison-shopping. I just want to get out of this dump.

—We have class.

—But one pill every day, they accumulate! Aren't they effective for at least thirty-six hours? You might kill me that way. In ten days, I will get effectively fifteen days' worth, in thirty, forty-five, so fifteen extra doses!

—You know, Gospodin David, this is very good news for me. We are starting this import business, and now we can sell the pills on the internet and in stores. What is the fair price, do you think? Maybe two pills for five dollars? That is very cheap, ten times cheaper than what you can buy in regular pharmacy. You have no idea what this means to me! By the way, are you single? I have an innocent daughter.

—What does innocent mean?

—I can't guarantee. Perhaps you are looking for a bride?

—I am terrified of Russian brides.

—You may be innocent after all!

The warden stood up, walked to me, grabbed my cheeks between his palms, and gave me a firm kiss on the lips, like Brezhnev kissing Honecker in Berlin. His teeth were uneven; one cut into my lower lip, and another into my gums. There was a taste of garlic and tobacco. I pushed the warden away.

—This is wonderful news, Gospodin David. I'm going to make a lot of money.

—Sir, this is disgusting. Your tooth cut into my lip and it's bleeding.

—You are a gentle man.

I wiped my mouth again, and there was a trail of blood on the back of my palm.

—Do you have some disinfectant?

—Why, you think a little scratch can harm you?

—What if you have hepatitis?

—Who, me? I am healthy. And what are you worried about, that my tooth would carry viruses?

—Can I have some rubbing alcohol?

—We have better things than that. Here, have a shot of pertsovka.

I accepted the shot and rubbed it over my lips.

—You are supposed to drain it at once, said the warden.

—I know the custom, but I need to disinfect the wound.

—The wound. It's just a little scratch. All right, here's a glass for disinfecting and here's one for drinking.

—Ouch!

The alcohol would have hurt my lip enough, but the hot pepper in vodka really burned.

—Ouch? What does ouch mean?

—When we are in pain, we say that in English.

—Why not Oy? Ah? How can you think to make that tsch sound when you are in pain?

—I am not a linguist. We just learn to shout like that.

—I know vowels are good for crying, but consonants!

—What did you want to talk about? About erections?

—If the drug works on Americans, it will work on anyone. It could turn even middle-aged Americans into good husbands.

—Fine. Now you know. Am I free to go?

—I also wanted to talk to you about your accommodations. We have so much to talk about! Are you satisfied with them?

—No, I have to sleep on the floor. How would I be happy with that?

—For five thousand rubles a month, you can have a solitary cell. And for one thousand more, you also get a shot of vodka for breakfast every day.

—Where would I get the money?

—You are a rich wine importer, correct? Perhaps you want to import Viagra and Cialis to New York and Chicago? It would be very profitable for both of us.

—I am not a wine importer.

—You don't need to deny it. Call up your friends, or we'll take a trip to the bank and you can draw money with your credit cards. Then, with some cash around, you will live like a prince here—your stay will be so pleasant you will not want to leave.

—How much would I have to pay to be released?

—I am not in charge of that, but while you are here, I can help you be comfortable.

———

We took a trip to the *bankomat*. The warden drove a black BMW, with a gold-inlaid mini icon, Lady of Kazan. Didn't the BMW in which I rode last have the same icon on the dashboard?

When we got out, I examined the bumper. It was indented— maybe from impact with a human skull? How many BMWs had the same icon and the same indent?

—How did you damage your bumper?

—I woke up one morning and there was this damage, but it's bound to happen sooner or later, the way people park around here, so why worry about it? Sooner is better than later. Anyway, what's it to you?

—When did you buy this car? Did you buy it used recently?

—What do you think of me? That I am such a loser that I couldn't afford a new car?

—Do you have friends? I mean, did you lend it to someone? This looks like the BMW that ran over the last Georgian wine importer, with me in the passenger seat, by the way.

—You got some balls, Gospodin. But that's good—may be a by-product of Chinese Cialis. The product proves to be overall *otlichni*. Gives you wood and balls. My friend, we are doing beautifully.

The warden tapped me on my shoulder powerfully, almost knocking me down.

—Would you like a little smoke?

—Smoke of what?

—Of Peter, my friend. Like Petersburg. That means a little Chi-cha in a Turkish joint along the Moika.

—Oh, no.

—Suit yourself. You could have had a wild night with some stoned Russian beauties, a night of freedom.

—That kind of illusion has cost me too much in this city.

—But now you are enabled, with my medicine. You would shine.

—Fuck you.

—You know, I like you.

—You should be behind the bars. You are a bunch of assassins.

—Takes one to know one. You are one of us.

—I refuse to be.

—Refusenik? Maybe I should decrease the dosage. You are aggressive.

—Aggressive for noticing the dent in your aggressive car?

—Nicely put. You are doing well. We were worried that you weren't talented enough.

—Who is we?

—Now, don't prove our suspicion, that you are not. . .

—Not what?

—Well, that will be another conversation.

CHAPTER THIRTEEN

I'm tempted to buy the rights to a life

AFTER A WEEK in the solitary cell, I had a distinct impression I was going crazy. Now impressions by their very nature should be hazy, but mine was sharp. For entertainment, all I could read was *Crime and Punishment* in Russian. I would have preferred some other book, but the classic was a patriotic book at Kresty. For years at the end of the nineteenth century, the library contained many copies but no other book. It was a practical joke played on the prisoners.

The warden, when I begged him to bring me something else, got me a copy of *Notes from the House of the Dead* and The New Testament.

—Why not the Old, it has better stories?

—Are you bored? Drug Popov asked me.

—There's nothing to do here. Could I rent a laptop to write something, just so I don't go completely insane?

—No, you can't have a computer, but I can get you, for a thousand rubles, a notebook and a pen. You can write letters and mail them, you can write your will and we can get a notary to seal it. Have you written your will?

—No, no will.

—You are rich, and you have no will?

—I am not rich and I have no will.

—Include me in your will! Maybe your dacha outside of New York?

—Right. Then my life would be short indeed. Anyway, I don't have a dacha.

—No dacha? You don't have to hide it from me. Nothing will happen to you. But, you know, there's a trial awaiting you, and I don't know what the judgment might be. Maybe life in prison?

—I should be tried in America.

—But for assassinations, I don't see how it would be any better in America. There, you might be executed. Capitalist capital punishment. We are not so barbaric—we have no capital punishment. You are in a bad situation, my friend. I think there is a way out. If you give us two hundred thousand Euro, we can let you go. We will not worry whether you killed two importers.

—Where would I find the money? And what would guarantee that if I paid you that much, you would let me go? You might keep me here as a cash cow.

—Once you paid the ransom, you could go back to America and become my business partner. Let me assure you, importing Cialis should be a much better business than importing Georgian wine. Soon you'd make four hundred thousand dollars, and you'd be ahead.

After the conversation, I kept thinking. Maybe I should raise 250K to buy back my freedom. How to do that? I had liquidated my retirement savings, but I did have an apartment in Inwood, valued at 350K. So the thing to do, probably, would be to have someone whom I trusted in NYC sell the apartment for me. Now who would that be? And what would happen once I got back to the city? I would be homeless—or anyway, forced to rent. What to do? Maybe I would manage to get out of prison . . . maybe someone would intercede for me? Who would that be? US ambassador? God? Or my ex? Ex-God,

ex-wife? Something ex should become current, so my ex-freedom
would be freedom again. I had a few days to make up my mind about
what to do.

While overdosing on the cumulative effects of Cialis, I thought I
could write a Russian story, maybe about Lenin's cat or about Rasputin's mysticism. I got blisters on my fingers from gripping the pen. I
could never develop the light touch on the paper to fly over the page,
and instead I pressed as though making ten indigo copies.

I jotted a story about Rasputin's conversion experience, which
consisted of being beaten with a lath of wood from a fencepost he
was stealing from a prosperous peasant. When the peasant, who
was even sturdier than drunken Rasputin, whacked the drunk over
the head, the drunk suddenly had a revelation and begged to be hit
again, in the name of the Lord, and in ecstasy of pain he had a vision
of peace and infinite copulation.

I was tempted to write a novel about Rasputin, but I would have
needed to get my hands on several biographies of Rasputin. It might
not be a bad idea to write an alternative history of Russia according
to Rasputin. One thing that I remembered from reading a Rasputin
biography was that unlike many Russians he was not a Slavophile
and he didn't think going to war to save the little Slavic brethren,
the Serbs, was worth the trouble. He had twice interceded to prevent
Russia from entering the Balkan wars before, and the only reason he
hadn't interceded in July and August to dissuade the Tsarina and the
war hawk duke, brother of Nicholas II, was that he'd been bedridden
after a superficial knife cut in Siberia. A peasant woman had tried
to stab him in his native village with a small kitchen knife, and this
nearly immortal man had almost died from the little cut. Rasputin
would have perhaps prevented World War One if he'd been in St.
Petersburg at that time. Without World War One, Hitler would not
have risen to power on the wings of German anger and humiliation

after France dismantled the coal mine industry in Germany to collect the exorbitant war damages, and if Hitler had not risen to power, maybe World War Two wouldn't have happened, and there would have been no Holocaust. It was possible that that one little wound on Rasputin's abdomen resulted in forty million deaths. Yes, why not write a novel about the pacifist maniac, who could have saved the world but instead contributed to sinking it. Without Rasputin's madness, perhaps the Tsarist system would not have collapsed, Communism wouldn't have happened, there would have been no Cold War, and the world would be simply an investment bank paradise, with a few fat cats skimming the cream until all the milk of the world turned into curdled water . . . Oh, who the hell knows what the world would be, but it would certainly find a way to rot and burn. Maybe there are no accidents in history; well, that's one school of thought, but I think there are accidents. In my personal history, for example: if I had fallen in love with the French culture as a child, reading Alexander Dumas, then indeed I would have become a wine importer. Or if I hadn't taken that dumb ride, standing on the curb waving down cabs, I wouldn't be in this idiotic prison. But if I was being framed, they, whoever they were, would have found a way of landing me in the prison anyway.

As I mused on how to continue the story, the warden visited me and said, —You still look bored.

—I would love to spend time with people, listening to Russian. I need inspiration and madness.

—You know the prices for the group accommodations?

—I thought that was for free. And I've already paid for the solitary confinement.

—Every change costs. For three thousand rubbles we can transfer you to a cell with eight inmates.

—You mean, the cell where I was before.

—Yes, that one. Or another one like it.

—But that's absurd. Give me back at least two thousand rubles as I am freeing up the solitary cell, which you can sell to someone else.

—It's not my fault that you don't like the single cell, and you've already paid. It takes work to move you to another cell. Take it or leave it.

—What work? My walking a hundred yards? But can you get me to a cell with only three other guys, where I would have a bed of my own?

—That will be ten thousand rubbles a month. So, what do you say? You want to move?

—Yes, but six thousand rubles?

—This is not Apraksin dvor for you to haggle. These are standard prices. Here, have a shot of vodka, to seal the deal.

I drank a sip, and then another one.

—Oh, that's not the way you do it. Gulp it down all at once. If you hesitate with the drink, you hesitate with the deal, and if you hesitate, it's no deal. Here, have another one, and do it right. Good. And now sniff this slice of rye bread to prevent a hangover.

He handed me a slice of bread that was at least a year old, as hard as a floor tile.

—But this slice is too old.

—It's not too old. It still gives off that rye aroma, which prevents hangovers.

—It smells like a brick.

—Sniff it for good luck.

—If good luck smells like this, I am in deep shit.

—You are in deep shit. And now let's go for a ride. And don't try to run away or I'll shoot you.

I thought that if I ran away, the drunken warden wouldn't be able to shoot me. Nevertheless, I didn't feel like running. Where would I go? How would I cross the border? Perhaps I could live as an illegal alien. The amazing thing about Russia is that it has as many illegal aliens as the United States does. Many people from the satellite republics, the former USSR, treat Russia now as a financial paradise, where you can actually get paid for work. There are even unregistered expats from Eastern Europe, and some expat Eurotrash and Ameritrash, who've figured out that living on fake documents is easier than renewing visas and getting repeated HIV and hepatitis tests. It's counterintuitive that Russia would be the land of the free, at least in my case, but . . .? Maybe I should become an expat. I could still draw money on my credit cards, max them out, and just disappear.

The warden smoked a cigarette and teetered next to the building with the street ATM, and I leaned with my left palm against the roughly stuccoed wall beside the machine. His eyes were bloodshot, slightly yellowish, as though stained by nicotine. This man couldn't shoot a fly, I thought. Well, yes, shooting a fly would be a greater achievement than shooting me. Whatever, I don't feel like running. Not today anyhow; I don't have a passport on me. He'll take me out again, and I'll make sure he will drink even more.

I took out nine thousand. The blue paper, impeccably new and straight, still smelling of ink, appeared in the tray with a shush. I handed the bills over to the warden.

—Beautiful. I suggest you withdraw some more.

—We can always come back for more if necessary. You won't just take it away from me?

—Why would I? I am an honest man, just trying to make a living, to feed my children and grandchildren.

—Grandchildren? Don't your daughters or sons take care of that part?

—You don't know the structure of the modern Russian family.

I withdrew twenty thousand rubles, in five installments.

—Good, now you will be more comfortable at Kresty. Hold on to your money.

—Actually, can I buy a phone card?

—I'll bring you one tomorrow. What system do you use?

—GSM.

—That's a good one. Putin's wife owns that company. It's my favorite.

The following day, with my card, I placed calls to the US Consulate. The Consul called me back and said he would work on getting me an extradition but in case of a politically motivated assassination, it was unlikely he could procure one.

Sam answered, —Hey man, I am at the airport about to fly to London. I can't do anything. You need better food?

—That would be nice. But it all costs money.

—I'll give Mario a call. He could bring you some dried fish.

—You mean the salty dried-up carcasses from the Baltic Sea that you and your buddies, when you drink, break with your hands and chew?

—Are they beating you?

—Nobody is bothering me.

—I'll write letters and make calls. It might be good experience being in Russian prison.

—You will write letters? That will take too long, especially from abroad.

—For now you can take it as research. If you want to write something, this seems like it would be a wonderful experience.

—I don't want to write from experience. I would prefer to write a novel about Rasputin, but I can't even get any books.

—You don't need to do any research on Rasputin. Anything you can say about him will be believable. It seems like a perfect place to do it. Maybe it should become a part of the Columbia writing program? We could reserve a dozen cells and charge extra tuition for the writers who want to have a genuine prison experience.

—Come on!

—When you get out, you want to be my partner in this? We could get American writers and jail them in Russia for a good fee and keep them there for an indeterminate amount of time on lousy food, without enough beds. That would solve a lot of problems for me. Are there any mosquitoes in prison? Things should be dire and terrible, and the students could complain if a meal turns out to be good and the bed soft and comfortable. You've just made my day.

—Wait a minute. Oh shit, I am already out of minutes.

Later on, talking with Drug Popov, I asked whether I could buy a few biographies of Rasputin to write a novel about him.

—Why would you want to do that? There are many novels about Rasputin.

—I have a lot of time. What can I do? Paint? Play chess? Study more history? What can I add to history?

—Why not write about someone more interesting, like Stalin?

—There are lots of novels about him. I want to write about Rasputin. Or Putin. Do you have any idea when they'll let me go?

—You better not write about Putin, what do you know about him anyway? And I am not the judge, how would I know?

—But from your experience, in cases like this one?

—I have no experience with economic assassinations. Sorry to tell you, your case is unique.

—But aren't most mafia murders economic assassinations?

—Probably, but we never get any mafia in here. Maybe you are the first mafia man we got.

—Don't flatter me. I am not that well-connected.

—If you want an interesting life for a novel, I could sell you mine.

—Your life?

—Rights to my life. For twenty thousand rubles I will talk to you for three days and three nights. That is how long it would take to tell you all the interesting things in my life, and you could tape record me, and then make a novel out of it, and I will sign the papers that I am not going to sue you for libel or theft of ideas. I will be happy to have all these memories in print before I go senile.

—No, thank you. I need to make something up, I don't need a real story.

—But you would like a biography with a real story of Rasputin.

—I need some grounding in facts.

—OK, I'll give you my facts and sell you my life for twenty thousand. You can shape it any way you like, add to it—but there's more there than anyone would believe.

—No, thank you.

—You are good at bargaining.

—When I don't want something.

—That is a good technique, to pretend you don't want it; even better, not to want it.

—Well, what is your story that you think it's so good?

—If you want any of it, pay.

—Why pay if I don't know what I'd get? First, a little sound bite? *Ugriz zvukyi.*

—Sound doesn't bite.

—I am translating an expression from English. Just a little notion what the story would be about. You can't sell something without describing the product.

—You are right about that. I was Putin's judo instructor and later his bodyguard. I know lots of things about Presidyent.

—How come you don't have a better job now?

—I am too old and out of shape. He's a judo black belt, and his standards for bodyguards are high. He personally tests them to make sure they are skilled and fit. As soon as he saw that I had some flab above my belt, he fired me. He hates lard.

—Hum. But for a novel, you need to write about someone likeable.

—Putin is likeable. He tells jokes and swears like a cab driver.

—Don't mention cab drivers to me. Likeable, like Stalin? Stalin told jokes and talked dirty. Putin seems a bit bland and hard to read.

—Oh, you are wrong about that. He is a great conversationalist. When he drank beer, he used to be brilliant. Especially if you mentioned East German female swimmers, you couldn't stop him.

—Did Putin give dope to the girls? East German swimmers were on steroids.

—He deflowered half of the Olympic team. For twenty thousand, I will arrange an interview with Putin for you so you can ask him such questions if you dare.

I scratched my scalp, an itchy spot, which worried me because it might be psoriasis or skin cancer, but how would I check that now? The idea that I could perhaps see Putin struck me as preposterous. No, this joker is making it all up. On the other hand, this is St. Petersburg, and Putin was hanging out in the martial arts clubs; maybe Comrade Popov is telling me the truth? Wouldn't it be scary to see Putin? I had met Clinton and I found Clinton's charisma scary.

—You are interested, I can see that. Think about this. If you don't want to write about me, you might have the first authentic novel about Putin, with many real insights and details. The price remains the same.

———

Several days later, the warden came to my cell and said, —You must come out. I have spoken to Presidyent. He doesn't want you to write a novel about him. You are forbidden to do it. I hope you haven't written a word about him?

—No, of course I haven't.

—*Pravda?*

—But if I leave Russia, I might.

—If.

—But why wouldn't he want me to write about him?

—He says that a foreigner, especially a non-Slav, could never understand the Russian soul and shouldn't write about a man of the people.

—But I am half Slovenian.

—We thought you were Jewish.

—You can be both Slavic and Jewish.

—You aren't good enough to write about him. He wants someone famous, like Dan Brown. He would prefer Milorad Pavić to do it. He already asked Solzhenitsyn, but Solzhenitsyn said he would like Putin to spend a fortnight with him in a monastery fumigating before he could write a biography.

—How would he know I am not good enough? I've published a story online about Milošević.

—Yes, he is aware of that. He read it. He says it is unconvincing, and you don't write with enough warmth and sympathy for Milošević. You make him a flat character. Your Milošević is more of a pancake than a person.

—How would you know?

—It's in your file.

—Why would I write with warmth about a mass murderer?

—Why not? Dostoevsky wrote with warmth about Raskolnikov, a double murderer. Raskolnikov killed two old women. How much warmth does that warrant? Yet Dostoevsky makes us tremble for him.

—Can I talk to Presidyent? I've written a better story, about Rasputin.

—I wouldn't be so sure.

—Why do you say that?

—Well, the Presidyent has read it, and he thinks it sucks.

—He can read through walls?

—While you were taking a stroll in the yard, I photocopied your story—it's in your notebook, it doesn't take a genius to do it, and I faxed it to him.

—Don't I have the right to privacy?

—Not in prison, my friend. We need to know what our prisoners are thinking. That's why we encourage the prisoners to keep diaries. And whatever work you do here, it all belongs to us. To me, to be exact.

—And he already read it?

—Yes, he's a genius. He can read two thousand pages an hour, faster than John F. Kennedy. By the way, what does F stand for? Fred? Frank?

—But Putin plagiarized an economics dissertation, the first forty pages verbatim.

—You have a proof of that?

—It was in the newspapers—for example, *St. Petersburg Times*.

—Oh, *St. Petersburg Times* is a right-wing publication catering to Americans, Canadians, and Israelis. How do you know he didn't write it first and then shared it with the American economist? Maybe the American stole his ideas, and they were so good that he immediately *poluchil* Doctorate. If I was you, I'd listen to Presidyent Putin. If he thinks you shouldn't write, you shouldn't write.

—I didn't know he was interested in writing.

—Spies are natural novelists. They plot everything. They know how intrigue works. Don't get me wrong. He doesn't think you are hopeless.

—There could be several novels about Putin. Maybe a trilogy? Putin's judo youth, Putin in DDR, Putin in Grozny. Can I talk to him?

—He is busy at the moment, traveling to China, and then to Croatia, where he's buying an island and a lake. I think he plans to retire there.

—Such powerful people never retire. Only Emperor Diocletian retired—and he moved to what's now Split in Croatia.

—Retiring on the Adriatic is an option. And Castro is going to retire as well. The two of them might share a small island off the coast of Cuba.

—What island? Turks and Calicos? He will visit me to breathe some warmth into my fiction? He seems the last person on earth to deal in warmth, other than Gazprom kind of warmth. Maybe he wants to hire me as a ghostwriter?

—He is coming to the prison anyway. He takes a strong interest in handling crime, to make sure that no real criminals go unpunished.

—I am not a criminal.

—He will determine that. One look into your eyes, and he will know everything about you. He will know whether God likes you.

—What if he gets the wrong impression, that I am guilty?

—Maybe he'll send you to a worse prison. He is very fair. By the way, do you have any more thoughts on how to export and import Cialis?

I was agitated. I would be seeing the most powerful man on earth. Could I be hanged? There's no capital punishment in Russia, so no, that wouldn't happen. But then, is that true, no capital punishment, when so many people get assassinated in the streets?

CHAPTER FOURTEEN

Is this liberation?

PUTIN STOOD in the circular atrium, and prisoners in cages on four floors gathered and cheered. Was it possible, the President is popular even among prisoners? Putin wore a blue suit, and his bald cranium and blond hair shone; there was an amazing radiance emanating out of him, and it occurred to me that perhaps there was no Putin standing there, but his likeness projected in 3-D; but where would be the projectors to create this illusion?

Putin, as though to dispel such doubts, shook hands with several prisoners so vigorously that they winced and gasped in pain, and he asked each one what crime brought him there.

—Stealing cars? You deserve to be here, and when you come out, don't steal anymore. Thieves are intelligent people. In the new economy, you can use your intelligence and make an honest living. Wouldn't it be better to be a car salesman?

—Yes, Gospodin Presidyent, it would be much better. I always thought so, but I didn't know how to start up the business. I'd need a startup capital to buy a few cars to sell, then buy more, sell more . . . I was working on the initial inventory.

—The cars don't have to be yours—you can deal for a carmaker, Volga for example.

—Do they still make those? I will try.

—Not only try, but succeed. Trying is not good enough. We want success, *pozhalusta!*

—And you, you killed your wife's lover? With an axe? That is horrible. Maybe you should have loved her and she'd have no need for a lover. You drank too much vodka and couldn't get it up?

The prisoners cheered, —Bravo, Presidyent!

—You are lucky, Putin resumed, that we have no capital punishment in this country. Maybe that should change. We have overcrowding in prisons, and it's too expensive to run them. And some people, like you, don't deserve to live. In America, they still have capital punishment and they say it costs two million dollars to execute someone. That is silly. A good bullet, that's all it would take, is a few rubles.

He shot a chilly look at the tall and stooped man, who was shivering either from fear or MDR TB (or both; the two are not exclusive). The man's blue lower lip, with a yellow sore in the left corner, trembled.

Putin's lips grew even thinner than they naturally were.

—We'll take care of him! shouted a husky bald man with a tattoo of Stalin on his head.

—No, you won't. Putin's eyes darkened as he focused on the tattoo. —You better not touch that man. I know you think it would please me if you strangled him, but if anything happens to him, more will happen to you. *Alles klar?* (Apparently when the president grew excited, he could slip into German.)

—Da, Gospodin Presidyent. You have read my mind. I did want to kill that man for you, but if you say . . .

—And why do you have a tattoo of Jugashvilli on your neck?

—You mean Stalin?

—Yes, *durak.*

Putin grabbed the man by the hand and flipped him—300

pounds flew over 130 like a feather in the wind, and landed like a sack of potatoes, against the ochre bricks of the wall and smoothly finished gray cement which looked like a frozen river. Putin waited till the sack of earth would become semiconscious, judging by two swimming bloodshot eyes opening up, and resumed his tirade:

—He was from Gori—burn—and should have stayed there! The name of the town says plainly what it shall do. I see, your tattoo is singed into your skin. At least you got that right. But don't touch that sick man. He is sick old Russia, a sort of saint with an axe.

Putin looked at the tall man who had turned light green in his face, and he said to Drug Popov: —*Tovarish*, take this man to the hospital—the Marine Hospital on Liteny—and ask for a contagious disease specialist to treat him with the best round of anti-MRD.

—But I am not ill! the man spoke in a phlegm-laden voice.

—By the sound of it, you have some serious sputum . . . Tovarish Popov, bring a white handkerchief.

Putin looked up at the tall man, the way one would look at a spruce spent by acid rain, and shook his head. Putin's eyes grew shiny with undropped tears, and of course, he didn't drop them (neither the eyes nor tears), and he said, Why did you use an axe?

—I read Dostoevsky.

—But the axe was applied on women there.

—Killing women is cowardly. I had the choice of splitting my wife's skull or her lover's.

—Excellent choice. I agree. However, you should have given him an axe too, to have a fair fight.

—He did not deserve a fair fight. I would have won anyway.

—You are still a slimeball, you understand that? And if you have TB, God has given it to you, and you deserve it. Now, pray for redemption, and He will help you get healthy. I think you have had the precisely right measure of punishment and suffering.

—Oh, thank you, Gospodin Presidyent!

I marveled. This diminutive man emanated a huge charisma and extraterrestrial confidence, aware that all his sinews and muscles aligned perfectly to generate maximum destructive potential. You cross this man's path, and you shall be strangled. And if he couldn't strangle you, he will send an assassin for you.

—Putin shook hands with me and looked up.

He was only five-five, slightly taller than Beethoven and slightly less angry. On television, he looked taller. I was nearly a head taller than the leader of the new world order. Yet the height didn't give me a feeling of superiority. Putin gazed into my eyes without blinking; muscles on his jaws popped as he pressed his teeth firmly. His handshake was amazingly limp. He gave me a dead mackerel handshake. I was ready to do some bone-crunching, to prove that I too had energy. He half smiled with his thin lips and shielded eyes. I was about to withdraw my hand from the handshake which had been going on a little too long. Putin's hand was cold, as is often the case with men who have an excellent and efficient cardiovascular system. Our hands bobbed up and down, and then, Putin squeezed my hand, turned around swiftly, and flipped me over his head and landed me on my feet.

I had no time to think or react.

—Just a little judo handshake, a test to see whether you are familiar with the martial arts.

—Very impressive, I said.

—Your physical guard, however, isn't. And what are you here for?

—False accusations. I did nothing.

—Nobody is here for nothing. There is no such charge. What is the charge against you?

—That I killed two Georgians: one, a mineral water importer, and the other, a wine importer. Actually, both were wine importers, and one dabbled in minerals on the side.

—And you didn't?

—No, Sir Presidyent. I haven't.

—I am sorry to hear that.

—To hear what?

—That you didn't eliminate two Georgian businessmen.

—I certainly haven't.

—Let me gaze into your soul for a second.

Putin got closer, put his hand on my belly, the soft area above the belt, an inch of spillover generosity of life, and he looked up. Strangely enough, or not so strangely, due to the Chinese contraband, I had to reckon with an erection.

I looked down, but not in the psychological sense, but rather awkward, stilted, literally stilted as though my legs were too long and wooden. I could fall from the heights, nay, I would, I will, the grammar will have failed. Putin's eyeballs were absolutely white, no alcoholic relaxation of blood vessels there. They didn't swerve; the eyelids didn't blink.

Putin awaited my response. I knew that his gaze, representing the mineral resources of the north, could not be ignored. My eyes could focus; my gaze shifted to Putin's ears, to the wall bricks, to the tip of his nose . . . my eyeballs positively oscillated.

—Yes, I see. You did eliminate two businessmen. That is truly fantastic. You are only a tourist in our country and you are improving it. You should be our national hero.

—You are messing with me.

—You shall come with me to Petrodvorets for a celebration. How would you like to work for me?

—But can I be freed from this prison?

—That's done. You are coming along with me.

CHAPTER FIFTEEN

Putin invites me to join the Russian plutocracy on one condition

THE CONVERSATION CONTINUED at Petrodvorets, in Peter the Great's study, near his tall bed and tall boots. It struck me as a strange turn in Russian history that after a giant founded modern Russia, such a short man should be leading it. I'd read a theory that at the beginning of each century, Russia takes a new course of political action, which determines the whole century. Seven-foot-tall Peter the Great founded the city in 1703; Tsar Alexander II defeated Napoleon in 1812 and introduced major reforms; Revolutions of 1905 and 1917 brought in the era of communism, and now, the year 2006 . . . Putin's oligarchy, or rather oiligarchy.

—So, here's my offer. If you follow it through, I will give you a square kilometer of beach property on the Lake Baikal right next to one of my dachas.

—I've never made it that far and the current airfares in Russia are outrageous. Why is that? The Russian gasoline prices are low and the airfares are high.

—Our airlines have to make up for losses incurred during the years of ridiculously low prices and save up to buy new planes, mostly Eurobus.

—Why not Russian-made planes? And what's wrong with Boeing?

—At the moment German engineering is more reliable and consistent. Can't trust Americans. Lufthansa has never had a crash. We need to rebuild our infrastructure, and then we'll make the best airplanes in the world.

—I won't be able to afford these airfares, so what's the point of having a far-flung dacha?

—Don't worry about that. You will fly first class if you do what I tell you. Lifetime subscription to first class. Go to Tbilisi and meet up with the Georgian president. As an American wine importer, you will have easy access to him.

—I am not a wine importer.

—You are. If you weren't until now, I tell you, you are now.

—You want me to negotiate for you?

—You obviously don't like Georgian competition, so it should be a pleasure for you to thwart them.

—Why don't you like Georgia? Wasn't your grandfather a personal cook to Stalin?

—He cooked a few meals for Stalin. How do you know that? But, you know, Stalin deliberately destroyed Petersburg. He let the Germans encircle it and choke it.

—And you resent not Germany but Georgia for it?

—When you meet with the Georgian president, drink with him. And he will get terribly drunk, and you can push him off his balcony at his country retreat. Or put some poison in his wine.

—And what will that accomplish?

—Without him, Georgia will give up the idea of NATO. Georgia won't mess with Ossetia.

—And what will happen to me? They will execute me in the public square?

—No, they are eager to prove they are a democracy. They have no capital punishment.

—They might shoot me on the spot.

—They might.

—That doesn't sound good.

—By the time the poison finishes him off, you would be back in Moscow.

—Or New York?

—Or New York. But you'd be safer in Moscow. You will be enjoying the Baikal. We can change your identity, get a Russian wife, and you can have a beautiful family. It is not too late yet. You are forty-eight?

—Turned forty-nine yesterday. I'd rather go back to New York. By the way, I've just got divorced, and it's too soon for me to remarry.

—Why go back to America. What is there? Shopping malls, obesity, parking lots, and rehab centers.

—What if I don't do it?

—By the way, what do you have against the Georgian wine dealers?

—I haven't done anything against them. It only looks like I did.

—Don't tell me that. You are obviously aggressive and enterprising. You could invest in Russia. Our markets have gone up 100% two years in a row while yours have been slipping. Come, join the country of the future. *Strana vazmoshnostei.*

—Sounds similar, like what we say in America, the Land of Opportunity. Is that a plagiarism?

—It's better, the Land of Potential. Powerful. Everything is possible in Russia. Power is better than opportunity. Opportunity is for weaklings.

—That sounds crazy—it's such a rigid country.

—Is it? Let's compare it with America, which has basically tried only one system, capitalism. In Russia, we are willing to try anything. We had tsardom. We made communism almost work. We tried anarchy and chaos, and then oligarchy; if Solzhenitsyn and his followers had their way (he's just too old), we'd have tried theocracy; and now we have the market economy and democracy and theocracy. If that fails, we'll try something else. And what will America try? Same old two-party system, which is just one party, Republican. Even when Democrats win, it's all Republicans. Trust me. We have a real democracy.

—Well, sir, what kind of democracy is this, may I ask, my being in prison as an innocent. I was merely picking up a cab ride, and the demented cabby ran over the Georgian pedestrian. Why would I be jailed—and the driver not?

—You are changing the subject. And you don't need a trial. You are free. Why talk about the past? There's only future. You are selected for a beautiful future. You will become an honorary citizen of Russia.

—All I see in Russia is the past.

—We are a young country, and the future is ours. We are number one in gas, wood, most metals, and oil.

—Saudi Arabia is the number one in oil.

—If you don't count the Arctic and Antarctic oil.

—But that doesn't belong to Russia. And is it exploitable?

—Yes, it does. We have staked our claim and put up Russian flags on the ocean floor below the ice. We are the number one in oil.

—The world is also about the people.

—We are the smartest mathematicians, computer programmers, and engineers. And even politicians.

—But you have suffered from the intelligence drain and beauty drain for decades.

—No more. They are now coming back, and soon we'll be letting superior and aggressive people, like you, immigrate. That will offset the decline in natality. You have no reason to go back to America. What have you there? Thirteen-trillion-dollar debt, and nine trillion extra pounds on human bones.

—Oh, you are exaggerating. Let's see, three hundred million Americans, with thirty pounds extra on the average per person, that is only nine billion extra pounds, and if there are 333 million Americans, there would be ten billion pounds of extra flesh.

—So that's what you call human resources in America? Ten billion pounds of lard. Can you imagine how much global warming the extra matter with its physiochemical processes produces? And just transporting that mass all over the globe in airplanes and cars—you can imagine the math.

—But here, you have nuclear radiation everywhere, and men live to be only fifty-nine on the average. In America, most people now can count on living to be ninety or perhaps a hundred with the improvements in medicine.

—You call that life? People ambling along with technological aids and federal money. That's your problem too. Don't you think it would be better if all the ill and unfit people died at the age of fifty-nine? By the way, you are maligning us. It's sixty-three by now, for men. Women, much higher, but I forgot their stats. Anyway, check out this little document. Putin pulled out a Russian passport and handed it over to me. —Open it!

A picture of me in a blue shirt stared out of the pages glumly. David Dvornik.

—Good name for you, isn't it?

—But what good is the Russian passport, when you can't travel on it abroad unless you get visas?

—That will change. Pretty soon you won't need visas to go to EU, you'll see. After your trip to Tbilisi, you get this passport and a villa. Where do you want it? Baikal? Hvar?

—Can I become a citizen without killing a president? I've never heard of such a citizenship test. I pondered the assignment. —How will I get to him?

—Easy. He loves America. He wastes his time watching the NBA via satellite. If you don't get to him, I will invite someone else, from America, to organize wine and mineral water exporting.

—You have his email address?

—I'll give you his personal cell phone numbers. And the US Embassy in Moscow could help you as well. Learn how to use your connections.

—Why would Saakashvili answer random calls?

—The US ambassador will be impressed by your story of mistreatment in the Russian prison system, and you will be his human rights pet.

—You know, I'd rather not kill anybody. Could I just interview you and publish your biography?

—There are already way too many biographies, and they are all boring. Write a novel, make me a hero who brings down the DDR. You know I did. They were becoming a little too uppity. But that didn't end well, as the Warsaw Pact fell apart.

—And you'll help me do the research?

—Why would I? Just get a bunch of books and read up on me. And now you've already met me, that should be enough.

—I don't get it. What's your obsession with Georgia? Do you know the song "Georgia on My Mind" by Willie Nelson?

—Ray Charles! Putin responded. —NATO embracing Georgia reaches deep into the Russian sphere—it's even worse than Cuba being a sore in the NATO hemisphere. Remember how the United States went ballistic over that one. And we should take the invasion calmly? US is threatening to invade Georgia. I have to beat them to it. *Verstehst du?*

—*Ja, ich verstehe.*

—Where have you learned German?

—Well, mostly like you, in East Germany, where my father worked as an economic advisor when I was a kid.

—Ach, *es ist so schoen Deutsch mit dir zu sprechen.* Putin put his hand on my shoulder, and said, —You will be my guest for a couple of days. My daughters speak better German than English, and they'll love the opportunity to practice German.

—But I am not a native speaker.

—All the better. Foreigners who learn German speak it more clearly than the natives. You will be a fine German tutor.

—Is that my job then? How old are they?

—One of your interim jobs. Don't pretend you don't know.

—Actually, believe it or not, I had no interest in you and I know very little about you. I don't follow yellow sheet pages. I know nothing about your kids. High school?

—No, they study at St. Petersburg State.

—So, they hang out in Peter? I might have seen them in the streets?

—Improbable.

—How do they study there, then? In an underground bunker with Uzi-equipped guards?

—They take their classes online, and sometimes we fly in their professors to Moscow or to Lake Baikal for some catch-up instruction. I could hire you as well, to be their instructor in investment banking and German and English. Multifaceted, aren't you?

—Really?

—Just get me your transcripts, and we can certify you as a visiting professor at Gosudarstvenii Univerzityet. You could teach them how to short American stocks. Don't you think it's high time to short the whole country?

—I think you are right. It will take at least nine more years for the economy to recover there. I . . .

—I have consulted the best economic advisors, including Paul Krugman. Have you met him? We know you are going down. So, what do you think—an independent course in investing for my daughters, to start with, let's say, a hundred million dollars each? One could short General Motors, Citibank, and GE. What do you think?

—I am impressed!

—Good, have a glass of fine Georgian red, two hundred years old. A little preview of Tbilisi.

I drank out of a gold cup, which I could barely lift. Soon afterward, I fell asleep, hugging a strangely big cat, and I woke up as the cat licked me hotly.

CHAPTER SIXTEEN

———

I fraternize with another fan of the Ukrainian gymnastics program

My situation seemed too good to be true, or too bad to be true, depending on what aspect I considered. I had daydreamed that Russia would disappear and also that the USA would disappear. Wouldn't that be a John Lennon dream, to lose two superpowers and live and love in peace, except John Lennon disappeared in the USA. Why the hell did he buy a floor in a building of a war empire if he really loved peace? Anyhow, Russia, an evil twin, seems to be here—there and nearly everywhere—to stay.

I rubbed my eyes and faced the calm face of Vladimir Putin, with a monalisaic smile curving his lips slightly, and slightly more to one side than the other, but not as much of a tilt as you'd see in the extended Bush family, where the downward tilt to the right has become a genetic bias.

—*Guten Tag, mein Freund!* I am so glad to see you are waking up. We have in the meanwhile traveled to another location, far more modernized than Petrodvorets. You slept so well thanks to the Georgian wines that you didn't notice anything.

—*Ach, Guten Tag, mein Herr!*

I looked around a huge room with canaries and waterfalls and Pachelbel lovelorn music. Buffed-up red and black kittens rolled in the corners, playing with yellow-green tennis balls.

—Oh, what beautiful kittens you have! I said. They look enormous for kittens.

—Guess how old they are!

—Six months?

—Four weeks. These are Amur tigers.

—You mean, Siberian?

—No, Amur. I know, you like to call them Siberian but that's not accurate.

Putin scratched one of them under the chin and brushed it. The cub shone in the golden hues of light from hidden lamps.

—I feel like Alice in Wonderland.

—*Genau!* We used a bit of pharmacology on you, but you are not hallucinating.

—I thought we drank ancient wine from Georgia.

—Laced with beta blockers. We know the combination works for you.

—You could have handcuffed me and blindfolded me like in the movies.

—But this is much simpler. You don't know where you are. Nobody knows where this residence of mine is.

—And where is it?

—Do you think I would be where I am if I had the tendency to reveal secrets? And we could be in Moscow.

—I am confused. How could I get here and not know it?

—I am disappointed you are asking that again. One moment, deep prison, another, palace. Upward mobility, American style. Except it's better, it's *Ruskii stil!*

Putin placed a tiger cub in my lap. The small cub had huge paws, the shoes to fill.

—Pet him! Putin ordered.

I did. It was wonderful, silky, warm, muscular . . . I had to close my eyes to concentrate on the unique pleasure of discordant notes of size and cuteness.

—He looks happy and relaxed but he's not purring, I said. Can tigers purr?

—Yes, I'll show you. Putin put the cub in his lap and petted it. A loud buzz came out, a slower purr than in an ordinary cat, but it came out only when the cub was inhaling, in waves.

—How come it purrs only when inhaling?

—Exhaling is reserved for roaring. Now you do it.

The cub had his tongue sticking out between his canines. I petted his neck and throat but the cub didn't purr.

—You are not relaxed enough, Putin said.

—Well, it's kind of hard now, surrounded by dictators and tigers.

—Are you flattering me? I don't have that much power to be a dictator. I would like to be, who wouldn't, but I am afraid I am a democratic leader. And this is just a kitten. Anyway, there's a simple way to relax, just like the kitten did. Put the tip of your tongue between your teeth, don't bite, and let your eyelids droop.

I followed the instructions and continued to stroke the felicitous feline's throat and neck. The cub's throat vibrated slowly under my thumb.

—I love our tigers, Putin said. I have my own preserve.

—Aren't they better off in nature?

—It is nature, two thousand square kilometers. Otherwise, there are only about three hundred of them roaming around freely. People shoot them to sell to Chinese old men. Those billionaires believe that if they ate tigers' balls and penises, they could get it up.

—That's idiotic!

—And they will pay a hundred thousand dollars for one tiger. There are too many poachers out there. The poachers call tigers land rovers—because they can buy an SUV from a killing.

—And you can't stop them?

—I haven't figured out how to just yet.

—I thought you can do anything in this country.

—I can't send an army to patrol the forests—and with such a huge terrain, I'd need quite a few soldiers. And the soldiers with their equipment would scare off the wildlife and make things even more difficult for the tigers.

—Man, you are right, I said, as the cub licked the back of my hand, a hot raspy tickle. This is wonderful.

—Who are you calling Mann? Putin asked.

—Sorry, I felt chummy because of petting the kitten.

—Don't call me Mann again. I am not a pothead. Call me Gospodin President Putin.

—Why? We are having a good time, aren't we?

—I am not going to evaluate the times, he responded in Russian. I've had better ones.

—This is indeed Wonderland. Kitties are tigers and presidents are, the way Georgian President Saakashvili put in, Lilliputin.

Putin said nothing.

—Didn't he call you Lilli-Putin?

Putin leapt out of his tiger-hide armchair, a yard off the floor.

After the leap, Putin settled back in his armchair as though nothing had happened. And I wasn't sure Putin had leapt. Putin's muscles looked even more defined than before. And he spoke. –I am not a hedonist looking for good times, at least not with middle-aged bankers from New York.

—But I am not . . .

—Don't worry about that, I have plans for you. This is a business meeting.

—I am not a businessman.

—You can't fool me, Mann. Mann. That fits you, you know. You are going to be the primary Georgian wine exporter and importer.

—You actually believe that?

—You will go to Georgia and talk to Saakashvili. He will trust you. He will try to replace the business which I shot down, of exporting Georgian wines, and people in Germany and American Georgia will drink Georgian wines.

—How can you talk like that? Germans love French and Californian wines; they don't trust the eastern goods.

—Don't worry about Germans. *Drang nach Osten.* They always wanted the East, and we got it for them. We got them caged in with Gazprom. Their former chancellor Schröder is an employee of Gazprom, tenth in the chain of command, making some cash, better than he could do with Mercedes or Krupps. They will drink Georgian wines if I arrange it, don't you worry! And don't get too dreamy. You have a job to do, a very important job.

—What is that?

—To tutor my daughters in the stock market and German.

—But that is ridiculous! Can't you get au pairs from Hanover with perfect *Hoch Deutsch*?

—I am only kidding about the language. You are experienced. You can teach them investing. They have E*TRADE accounts, some play money, a million in each account. You've been a major Enron stock scam artist.

—Oh, please don't remind me.

—You mean, you didn't know you were running a scam?

—I didn't know it was a scam. It just seemed like energy was instant. You know, Tesla thought of wireless transfer of electricity.

—And so you had wireless transfer of stocks for old-fashioned wire-transferred electricity and sold tales of instant energy.

—Well, if Gore had won, we'd have had wireless transfer of electricity, bullet trains, and all.

—That wouldn't have been good for Russia. We need earthy energy, oil, gas, coal, that's what we sell. We don't sell the sky. Everybody has that. Why do you think Gore didn't win?

Putin chuckled.

—But why don't you hire Schröder to teach your daughters?

—His job now is too important to be sidetracked like that.

—And mine is not?

—And what is yours? To screw around and be a prison bitch.

—Touché! Drinking wine and selling it could be.

—Will be. You will go to Tbilisi in a month.

—For President Saakashvili?

—I wouldn't call him president. He's just some Soros stooge, a goofy student from Kiev and Columbia. You'll have fun with him. He believes that wine was fermented in Georgia seven thousand years ago, roughly around the time—or a little before—the earth was created according to the old interpretations of the Bible. He will tell you about the Georgian Ur-wine. And you'll drink with him some liquid crap, three hundred years old.

—You mean, as old as St. Petersburg.

—*Pravda.*

—I will drink to St. Petersburg, wine that was made at the same time as the rocks were dumped into the marshes to lay the foundation for the city.

—And when you are both happy, and when he's told you how great Georgia is, you will slip a gram of polonium into his wine.

—Where will I get it from?

—I shall give it to you.

—It's funny it's sounds like Poland. Polish poison?

—Madame Curie developed it in 1893 and named it after her home country.

—How does it work?

—It messes with the physiology of the human cell and the cells turn on themselves and commit suicide. Marvelous.

—But how can I carry it?

—In a tiny lead capsule.

—But isn't it highly radioactive?

—*Genau.* That's the point, *mein Freund.* After he ingests it, he will die within fourteen days.

—But how can I carry it and be safe? Won't it kill me or burn a hole in my skin?

—We'll put it into a lead capsule. Actually, a gold capsule. Gold is better than lead as a barrier.

—Won't it draw attention at the customs?

—We'll put it into one of these tiger cubs, and you will bring the cub along as a present.

—But how will I get it out of the cub?

—With a laxative.

—You mean, you'd make the cat swallow the capsule? In that case, the cat should vomit it.

—No, that might be too complicated. You could just stick the capsule up the cat's ass, and when you need the capsule, administer a laxative. But before that, for the flight, you should give the cat some constipation medicine.

—But it will be weird if I give the president a Siberian tiger. That's not what Americans usually give.

—Oh really? Aren't tigers all the rage among the rich Americans? What's the name of that circus clown who was killed by his pet tiger?

—OK, but if I go in a month, your cub will be getting too big to travel. What if he bites me?

—I have thought of that. Plan B is that you take your own cat.

—I don't know whether she survived my imprisonment. You know, I used to have a cute tiger-striped cat named Murmansk.

—If you agree to go to Tbilisi, I'll get you your *koshka*. You could always go back to Kresty.

—You are blackmailing me?

—No wonder America is in trouble, when even your bankers are so thick. I am not blackmailing you. It's either or, a clear choice.

—You have my cat?

—*Naturlich.*

Now I leapt out of my armchair.

—*Langsam.* I can show her to you via live security camera. Come here.

Putin opened a large Apple computer, and after a few clicks, a streaming video—two red and black cubs and a gray and black tabby cat playing soccer with orange ping-pong balls.

—Looks like her!

—It is her.

—But how did she get here?

—My agents rescued her from your apartment.

—How long ago?

—Right after your imprisonment.

—I thought you didn't know about me then.

—Here, won't you have a halbliter of Heffeweizen?

—If you will have one too.

—That I won't do. But don't worry: I have no reason to poison you. I drank only when I was in DDR; now I watch my waistline. Before I liked eight-packs in me, now I like them on me.

Putin peeled off his white T-shirt, tensed his torso, and thus displayed his serrated muscles.

—Funny, Bush doesn't drink either, and I can think of a few other leaders who didn't drink.

—I know who you are thinking of—and by the way, Gitler did drink beer all his life, as he thought it was the German national drink, something like kvass for Russians. And Paul Newman considers himself a teetotaler but drinks a six-pack every evening.

—How come you Russians can't pronounce H like G, Gitler, Golandia, Garvard.

—In German, I'll say it like the Germans do, and in Russian like us Russians.

—So you can make exceptions for kvass?

—Kvass has three percent alcohol content, in other words, like American Budweiser—although it contains even more calories.

—How about Bush? He doesn't drink but looks drunk all the time.

—You think Bush has a six-pack? I felt him. He's pretty soft.

—So, no competition for you?

—You think Russia would be doing so well if you didn't have a moron for president? Bush messed up the Middle East, burnt the pipelines, and quintupled the price of oil. And of course, that increased the price of natural gas, with a little help from the Ukrainian craniums.

—Yes, that's all true. This is suddenly a prosperous country, for some.

—Yes. You are invited to immigrate.

—I was considering it, but I just can't think like that. To begin with, I am trying to leave Russia, frankly speaking, after the Kresty incident.

—You can't worry about such a little detour. It will turn out to be the best thing that's ever happened to you. Do you love Russia?

—I used to.

—After you do what I am proposing, you won't have a place in the American society. Oh, here comes your Heffeweizen.

Suddenly in walked Yuliya, shimmering like gold.

Startled, I said, —You? How is that possible?

Putin laughed. —Nice! I knew we would like each other. I must admit I too have a weakness for Ukrainian gymnasts.

—Oh, Yuliya, so that's how you disappeared. What are you doing here?

—I am an au pair, like you.

—I am a man, I can't be an au pair.

—Why not? You can teach Putin's daughters German, I teach you Russian, and it's one happy polyglot family.

She lifted her arm with considerable effort and poured golden hissing liquid into a Czech crystal glass reflecting and refracting yellow hues from Yuliya's golden dress, two Amur—amour?—tiger cubs, tiger lilies in a golden vase, and several paintings of golden calves by Franz Marc.

—That must be Franz Marc, I said to Putin.

—It is.

—I've never seen this one.

—It's private.

—How did it get here?

—The Red Army officers brought it back from Berlin as a little recompense, to Kremlin.

—So, we are at Kremlin?

—Nothing that obvious. Maybe at one of my dachas.

—Some dacha with walls two meters thick!

—Beautiful, aren't they? Just touch the walls, smell them, feel them.

—They smell like river sand and catfish, in other words, like Petersburg. By the way, that reminds me of what Oscar Wilde said, *Bulk is the American canon of beauty.* I guess he could have said the same thing of Russia.

—Yes, multiply it by two and then you got it. We are double the size of America.

—You used to be 22,402,200 square kilometers when you had all those republics—2.3 times bigger than the States. Russia is 1.7 times the size of the United States.

—How do you remember that?

—I like numbers.

—You like Franz Marc? Putin asked.

—My favorite painter—wild, expressive, almost cubist, but better to say, elliptical, and yet always beautiful. Didn't he get shell-shocked in World War One?

—Not shell-shocked. Stimulated. Like Céline, who could finally write after getting a bit of shrapnel in his head. If you poison Saakashvili, maybe he'll become an artist. And the painting will be yours.

—You mean, if I stimulate Saakashvili. But how will I take the painting out of the country?

—You can't. It's our national treasure. It's yours only if you stay in the country.

—You mean, it won't actually be mine?

—Yes, it will be yours. Great art is real estate. You can't take a house out of the country, and why should it be any different with a precious painting?

—I could sell it if necessary.

—That would be rude. You don't sell gifts, especially not given by the President.

—What happens if I leave Russia? What do I do with the painting then?

—What's the point of leaving the best country in the world? You'll come back. Franz Marc will be waiting for you in an apartment—choose the location—in St. Petersburg.

—Not Moscow or Murmansk?

—There's only one great city in Russia. What's your favorite street?

—I'd say Griboedova, near the Kazan Cathedral.

—It's uncanny. We have the same tastes. I'll give you one three-bedroom penthouse.

—That's too good to be true.

—No, *mein Freund*, only the best things are true.

—I mean, how can all this be real?

Putin punched me in the abdomen so I doubled over. —Does this feel real?

—Agh, I am afraid so.

—Why afraid? By the way, if you are going to be my friend, you have to do two hundred sit-ups and one hundred pushups a day. I hate flabby people.

—I don't mind. I always planned to get into shape.

—It's not a plan, it's a lifestyle. Now, why don't you kiss Yuliya?

—Why, just like that, in front of you?

—She's your friend. You haven't seen her in a while. Greet her properly.

Yuliya nodded. She leaned over and poured one more glass of *pshenychanya* Baltika.

I stood up and kissed her cool cheeks. Her skin felt soft and thin.

Putin shook his head slowly. —You are trying to display manners? French kiss? *Mein Freund*, we are all beyond that. You like her, kiss her on the lips. She's been pining for you.

I kissed Yuliya on the lips, which were so cool that I wondered whether I was feverish or whether she was a few degrees cooler than normal. Maybe super-athletes cool off when not exerting?

—*Sehr gut*, said Putin. Yuliya will accompany you on your trip to Tbilisi as your wife. That will be more convincing than traveling alone like an American derelict spy.

—But she is not my wife.

—As a matter of fact, she is.

—But I haven't said yes. And if I have a Russian bride, won't it be suspicious? Well, she's Ukrainian.

—Same thing. Ukrainians are Ur-Russians. Everybody wants to have Russian wives and Amur tigers.

Putin shook off his suit sleeve to look at his watch. Of course, he had many other things on his mind, besides hiring me.

And I said: —So should they know I am coming from Russia? Wouldn't it look better and more convincing if I was coming from New York?

—You don't have to hide coming from Russia. You have been abused in Russian prisons, and that is a good credential.

—But how will they know?

—Easily. We'll give you typical Kresty prison tattoos, on your back and your arms.

—I don't want tattoos.

—Against your religion? No craven images?

—Tattoos contain metallic traces. I will never be able to have a proper MRI if I have a tattoo. You have many plans for me, too many. And you know, I don't want to be married again. One bad marriage was enough for me.

—You never said no. You have kissed the bride.

—But that's ridiculous! If everyone you kissed became your wife...

And I thought, I should get in touch with the warden and get a year's supply, as long as good sex lasts in an average marriage. According to an article I read in *Psychology Today*, love in marriage lasts seven years in Europe, three in the States, and one in Italy.

—You are a lucky man, Putin said. You wanted an apartment on Griboedova, Yuliya, Franz Marc, and another glass of *pshenichnaya* or single malt? You get all four wishes fulfilled, better than if you'd run into a genie.

Putin looked at Yuliya and his eyes flared up with pale blue fire, like a welding light. He reclined in his armchair and laughed. — Yulichka, give him another shot.

I put forth my crystal cup, and Yuliya produced a bottle of single malt, shimmering like gold, but clear like vodka, magnifying the purple emanations out of the Bohemian crystals. I wondered what the label was. La Gavulin?

Putin seemed to read my thoughts. —You want labels? It's not black label. You want gold with label? You Americans and your labels! Pure gold precedes labels.

—By the way, Putin said. This single malt is 303 years old. An ounce of it is worth as much as an ounce of gold, so drink it and be merry. Old Yeltsin gave it to me. He knew the whole story but forgot it as his brain had dried up.

—You aren't poisoning me?

Putin rubbed his hands as though they were chilly. —We could shoot you, burn you, dump you in a dumpster off Griboedova, anything you fear we can do . . . but we are treating you like a lord. You will be one of us.

Yuliya was helping herself to a little shot of the unnamed exotic Scotch single.

Putin was petting an adolescent snow leopard, who was growling rather threateningly.

—Can you believe the size of his tail? he said.

—What a wonderful creature. Where did he come from? You just had a little tiger there.

Putin thumb-nailed his nose as though in sympathy with Yuliya. —You are confused, David. You have, to put it rather curtly, the perfection of human evolution here in Yuliya.

—Not the snow leopard?

—The Amur tiger, provided there's a large enough ecosystem, is superior.

—To a Ukrainian gymnast after all?

—You can't compare. Both, fantastic.

My scalp felt electrified; Yuliya was passing her fingers through my hair, and her long fingernails scratched me lightly. Her noble-metal-wrapped hip rubbed my shoulder while Putin lectured:

—The genetic warfare of the East and the West has resulted in this rigorous gymnastic training, which is difficult to give up midstream if you are on top, as Yulichka was, and here she is, a supple example of ultra-limberness. If you are top ten in the world, about to go to the Olympics, in your prime, you don't just retire, as she did. It would be like my retiring now. Yes, I am in my prime, and it would be wise to retire. I did buy a couple of islands in Croatia and Greece, but I have no intention of going there.

Putin switched on a television set—from somewhere behind us was projected a beam of oscillating light which landed on the whitewashed wall of the underground chamber.

—*Stille*, Putin said. —I am addressing the nation live.

On the screen showed up Putin, addressing the nation as *Moyi druzya*, my friends.

—How can this be live? I whispered to Yuliya.

—It is, she said.

—But you are here, Gospodin Presidyent!

—Yes, I am here, and my double is talking at the Kremlin.

—So we are not at the Kremlin.

—This is my double, a few years younger than me and an inch taller. That leaves a better impression. And we could be at the Kremlin, St. Petersburg, Lake Baikal. You don't need to know.

—How can you trust him to talk?

—He's reading the speech.

—Can he do a good job? Aren't you afraid that it will turn out like that Brezhnev joke? The kind that got people imprisoned—maybe you even reported on people who told jokes when you worked for the KGB.

—I never worked for the KGB. They worked for me. Anyway, what joke?

—On his deathbed, Lenin summons Stalin. *Josef, I'm not sure you're the right man to lead the country after me. I don't know if the people will follow you.* Stalin responds, *Don't worry, Vladimir Ilyich. Half of the country will follow me, and the other half will follow you.*

—Oh, yes, that one. I made that one up and let it circulate.

—Really, I never noticed that you have a sense of humor. You always seem terribly serious.

—I have reasons to be serious. You know, even that idiot, Georgie Bush, is funny. He said he stayed away from Dick Cheney because he didn't want to be a lame duck president. It's easy to be funny. This guy is sharp. He can even improvise and answer questions and swear when necessary.

—How do I know that that's not the real Putin and that you aren't his surrogate?

—That's the beauty of it. You don't. Either way you are dealing with Putin, and your job and the rewards remain the same. By now it's all virtual reality, unless of course you get shot.

—But why would you have a double to work in public?

—Rhetorical. You have figured it out.

—No, I am asking.

—You are thicker in your head than I thought. I have a public persona, literally a double, as a decoy. There have been already fifteen assassination attempts on my life. The guards are so good they managed to thwart all of them before a shot was fired, but it would have made no difference. Only my double would have been killed.

—And that would make no difference to you?

—This is a risky job, and while I am brave, I am not going to play the Russian roulette, as I am not stupid. In fact, I am extraordinarily intelligent.

—Do you remember how Stalin sent assassins to poison or shoot Tito, and Tito sent a note to Stalin. *You've already sent more than twenty assassins. If you keep it up, I will send only one and that will be the end of the story.*

—I don't remember that. How old do you think I am? You will be the only one to do Saakashvili.

—Really? But if I remember correctly, in 2005 there was an assassination attempt on Saakashvili during Bush's visit to Tbilisi. A man threw a live hand grenade to the podium but it didn't go off. Vladimir Arutyunian was his name; sounds Armenian? Maybe he was nervous and he didn't throw well—the grenade deflected off a girl's head in front of the stage. Did you send him?

Putin smiled and gazed at me for a few seconds. –That's nice, the topic clearly interests you if you remember the names. But no, I'd never use such crass methods.

—A grenade worked on the Tsar Alexander the Second.

—You imagine I was involved in that too? Well, this grenade in Tbilisi didn't work.

—If I fail, you will send someone else?

—If you fail, I'll send someone else, or maybe I will send MiG jets to Georgia, but you can't afford to fail. And better living with chemistry, isn't that your American motto? Better death with chemistry. Polonium-210 will make it easy.

—The whole world knows that you are sharp. But why didn't you finish writing your Ph.D. dissertation but copied a chapter from a Princeton grad student?

—Case in point. I had better things to do. You think anyone reads dissertations? Everybody pays attention to bombed-out cities. Anyway, it wasn't me who copied and plagiarized anything; it was my double, without consulting me. And I told him to read and adapt a bit of Krugman—that *chelovek* is brilliant!—but he strayed and copied some bozo. By the way, I appreciate that you are frank with me. Most people—actually all of them—don't dare bring up this issue in my presence.

Putin slapped me on the shoulder. —So you are not a wimp after all. That is good, as you will need the balls in Tbilisi. But let's listen to what I am saying!

Russia has risen to the dominant role in the world as a superpower with the largest natural resources in the world. However, we are losing manpower, we are falling behind in our recruiting potential. We should be able to have an army of three million soldiers but can't even manage half that many, and why? I ask you why? There was no response from the audience, and Putin, on the screen, said, *Our women and men aren't making enough babies. The infertility rate is high because of drugs, poor nutrition, and mercury and lead poisoning, our heritage from the old days of mismanagement. But the greatest problem is immigration.*

—Immigration? I asked Putin. You plan to invite people from all over the world in?

—No, my friend, other than you. Listen. . .

We have, for at least a decade, allowed our most beautiful and fertile women to leave the country to produce strong young men for America, Britain, Germany, and Italy—in other words for NATO, which pretends to be our friend. We will make it much more difficult for the young women to leave; we need them here to make the new generation of soldiers for us. Moreover, we'll pay each couple thirty thousand rubles a year per child. Bearing children will no longer be a financial burden but a reward on all levels—you will know that you are strengthening Rodina, you will be getting a steady source of cash to buy better groceries than before, and you will be happy. You will not need to drink much anymore. I don't mean there will be another sukhoi zakon, as you all need to relax now and then. So that is our new immigration program.

—Emigration, he means, I said. In other words, *am strengstens verboten.*

—I mean immigration, Putin said. We need more babies to immigrate into life.

—That sounds like a sophism. You are kidding?

—Hush! Listen. Oh, the hell with it. Putin switched the TV off and looked dejected.

—What is wrong, Dedushka? Yuliya asked him.

—Oh, they've edited my speech. It was funny and brilliant, and earthy, with a nice joke, and now it's only functional. I had a few lively expressions, but the motherfuckers took them out.

—I thought it was a good speech, Yuliya responded. But, if you don't mind my saying so, couldn't you let Ukrainian women come here without a visa and stay on and make babies for Rodina?

—That is an excellent idea!

—And Ukrainian men?

—Oh, we can do without them. We have enough men power at home and if they happen to be lazy, there are enough virile visitors from all over the globe. You don't think I know what is going on, Putin said, giving me a rather cold gaze. —Anyway, my friend, I am not here to discuss fertility with you. Off you go.

—Where? I am not ready.

I felt like I was being kicked out and only now realized that I'd thoroughly enjoyed hanging out with the most powerful man in the world. What does that say about me?

—You are ready. Yuliya has everything for you.

—Even new passports?

—No, mein Freund. Your American passport is your trump turd. I have your Russian passport, which I'll give you later.

—You mean trump card?

Putin petted the flab above my belt. I was getting an erection again. So it was true, power was an aphrodisiac. Or it was still just Chinese Cialis?

—Here, take your cat, Tovarish Putin said. —She has eaten plenty, and you should be in Tbilisi within twenty-four hours. Here is some Benadryl to make her sleepy and perhaps it will subdue her allergies. Oh yes, a little iodine pill too, which helps to ameliorate the effects of radiation. You could take one too. Well, you'll take more than that, so you won't know where you have come from and how long it took to come out of here. *Horosho, mein Freund?*

Putin stood up, tiptoed, and planted a rather firm kiss straight onto my chin. While kissing me, Presidyent placed his thumb knuckle above the fourth lumbar disc behind my spine, and pressed sharply, so that I nearly doubled backward into a flip.

And that is the last thing I remembered of that soiree before regaining consciousness at Pulkovo Dva Airport.

CHAPTER SEVENTEEN

Yuliya and I on the way to Georgia.

YULIYA WAS GLISTENING in the sunshine and holding my hand, and in the pet carrier purred my trusting creature, Murmansk. It was the definition of happiness for me.

—Wait a minute, we are at St. Petersburg Airport. I thought we were in Putin's residence in Moscow!

—So did I, Yuliya retorted. But he hates Moscow and loves St. Petersburg, and he does what he wants. Don't you think he probably lives in Peter? Of course, he has a dacha near the lake.

—Which lake?

—Several of them.

—So where were we? What's your guess?

—What's yours?

—I'll have to think about it. Petrodvorets?

—That would make sense.

—There's a lot of plundered German art there in the basements. And not only that, Peter the Great was one of the tallest emperors ever. I mean, for God's sake, he was as tall as John Kerry.

—Who is John Curry if you don't mind my asking? An Indian TV cook?

—No, a Brahmin politician from Boston.

—Ah, so, upper-class Indian? He cooks well? They can marry?

—Yes, he can marry and did—a Heinz heiress, you know the family that makes tomato sauce.

—It sounds like a marriage of convenience. They can make great masala together.

—He could buy a lot of ketchup on his own, but he may have married for the sauce. Kidding aside, he's one of the smartest American politicians who should have become president of the United States . . . but for those voting machines in Ohio produced by a Serbian businessman with connections to Putin. Maybe it's Putin who prevented John Kerry from becoming President. Anyway, do you think it's possible that we were in the basement of the Winter Palace? He only pretended that we had left Petrodvorets. And so he could show us Franz Marc and other paintings.

—Maybe he'll tell us later, when we get back from Tbilisi.

—Yes, if we ever do. What if we hit it off with Saakashvili and end up living in one of his vineyards?

I chuckled—not a bad scenario, to retire in a Caucasian vineyard with a young femme fatale (to die for, or to live with, or to kill for... only the middle option seemed right). I am going to become a murderer now to make this dream true. And whose dream? And maybe it will be some kind of vineyard in Sochi, with sour grapes, mostly white wines, and I'll live with one of Putin's doubles or triples.

We walked to the narrow security gate. I took off my shoes, and said, —Wait a minute. This is my cat; she can't go through X-rays.

—*Konyeshna*, said a red-lipped policewoman.

Men in Russia, I concluded, don't work all that much, so most jobs are manned by women, and that included police jobs.

She took the green pet carrier past the gray plastic scanning gateway, on the right side, from my POV . . . and the security alarm went off nevertheless.

—What's that, sir? You have some radioactive metals here?

—Oh, I am simply a fat American who has just had a cardiac isotope test so I am still a little bit radioactive. Wherever I go, alarms go off.

—We get at least five such incidents a day, said another police-woman, a customs exit officer, who, unlike the more noticeable one, had no lipstick, no hourglass. —And do you have the papers?

—I have all sorts of papers.

—To prove that you had the medical test.

—I even have the papers proving that my cat has had a rabies shot. And a chip—with a frequency—so she could be tracked in Western Europe.

—Oh, what a lovely cat, the cop said, and petted Murmansk, who purred trustingly and blinked.

I thought, You striped opportunist . . . I believed you purred only for me, but go ahead, purr on, it's a great idea.

—Can I have her? asked one policewoman in a green uniform and a tilted Soviet-style cap, rather becoming on her sloppily yet fashionably streaked brunette turned blonde hair, which formed a letter C around her ears, with the lower C hairs sticking forward. She wore excessive rouge on her highly defined and wavy lips. The lips stiffened and shrank. Now they looked stern, extra creased, de-creamed. The police person who had metamorphosed into an MM for a few seconds returned to her official image.

—She's my pet! I said.

—I'll give you five thousand rubles for her. Six.

—No way.

—Or jail. Radioactive materials.

—That won't work, I said.

—It won't, Yuliya said. We should have diplomatic immunity. Scan our passports and read.

—You should have diplomatic immunity? the red lips annunciated ironically and swore.

—That doesn't sound like official Russian to me, Yuliya said.

In the meanwhile, her colleague, who had run the passports through the computer sensor, said, —Pass them through! She whispered something in her ear. Now her cheeks looked white and dusty. She too had a startling redness to her ruffled lips.

I smirked as we walked up to the second floor of the concourse, Murmansk purring in the green carrier bag.

—Isn't she like a snow leopard? I asked Yuliya. The long tail, a bit longer than the usual cat's tail. Putin pointed that out to me.

—You are right, it is.

—Yuliya, you are just cowed by Putin. Putin lover!

—So are you! Admit it, David. You like his power.

—Like is too simple. It's strange we both know him and we met just like that, by accident.

—Maybe it was fate? Maybe we were meant to be together.

—Meant by whom? Did you know of me before?

—No, but that Hungarian diplomat knew Putin from Germany.

—So you spent more time with the Hungarian than you let on.

—You are jealous! That's sweet.

We got on board Air France to Paris, CDG, where we would change to Tbilisi, as there were no longer any direct flights from Russia to Georgia. At the counter, the check-in person didn't ask for an extra fee for the pet.

—That's lucky, I said. Usually they charge for pets.

—What a pain, Yuliya said, not to have a direct flight.

—Perhaps not. We get a stopover for a day in Paris—chevre and red wine are waiting for us. And yes, garlic and cottage cheese.

Yuliya fell asleep and her forehead rested on the seat in front of her, which reclined back.

A frizzy-haired flight attendant with a nametag Mathilde—next to her not-fully-buttoned-up cleavage—asked me whether I'd like orange juice or water, and I said, —*Deux verre du vin rouge.*

—*D'accord.* What kind would you like?

—How many kinds of reds do you have?

She squatted revealing her thighs and stood up effortlessly and handed me two bottles.

—One for you and one for your cat!

It took me less than ten minutes to finish the two little bottles. It had been a long time since I'd had decent red wine. The ancient Georgian wine at Putin's was foul; he had probably given it to me as a practical joke. Maybe he had added some drugs which made the wine taste extra rotten.

Mathilde kept coming to my seat, and she petted Murmansk. Her fingers kept sliding from the cat's fur to the hairs above the knuckles of mine which sent shivers up my arms.

Mathilde went to the toilet and winked at me. I went in after her, and what hadn't happened in Russia despite all the teasing, suddenly happened. Thanks to my cat! Outside stood Yuliya, apparently waiting for her turn. She grimaced when she saw Mathilde walk out of the toilet as well.

Yuliya stayed in the bathroom for a long time, and I wondered what she was doing there. I was tempted to walk back and knock in case she had passed out, but just then she reemerged, with more lipstick and sharper eyebrows. She smelled like menthol and Bulgarian roses.

—Guess what? Good news, I am not impotent. I just checked.

—It's good news?

—When we get married, we'll have a great love life.

We spent the night at the Hotel Intercontinental near the Louvre. On the way to the elevators, Murmansk meowed from her duffel bag but we were not stopped by the sharply dressed butlers, who seemed more interested in standing up straight, like guards at Buckingham Palace, than in paying attention to visitors. Before giving Murmansk water to drink, I walked out to buy a petit sandbox. It took me an hour to find one. I was afraid to give her food, so I didn't.

Yuliya rebuffed my hands and wouldn't kiss me either.

—Aren't you coming with me to Tbilisi?

—Maybe, just to see it and compare Georgian restaurants there with the ones we have in Peter.

—Saakashvili loves Ukraine. He had great times in Kiev as a student. Who knows, maybe he even remembers you from the competitions—you were probably competing when he was a student.

—That is all possible.

—Do you know him?

—I don't know if I do.

—What an answer.

—I would know only once I began to talk with him. I don't always remember the faces but I do the feel of the communication.

—I guess you were a celebrity and knew a lot of people.

—Maybe.

—So please come along. That will make my job easier.

—Luckily, there are two beds in this room. But if you think I am going to forgive you, you are mistaken.

In the morning, we were both red-eyed.

—Your snoring really is horrifying, she said. You should get it checked with doctors—maybe they can cut out half of your throat for the airflow.

—You are looking at me as if you wanted to perform the surgery.

—That might be a cure for sleep apnea. And death would defi-nitely cure it.

—I see, you missed a career in medicine.

—I am still young, I could be a doctor.

—How about a wine importer's wife?

—You drink too much.

—Even for a Russian?

—Russians don't drink that much. They are so happy when they get a chance to drink that it looks like they are all terrible drunks, but I have read the stats. Russians are way behind the Germans, the French, even the English.

—What was all this about, your traveling with me? Are you just making sure I get on the plane?

—I'd like to do some shopping in Paris, and I have a couple of old friends in the city.

—Let me guess, diplomats?

—No, former gymnasts like me, a rock star, and sure, a dip-lomat.

—From what country? Hungary.

—Not Hungary.

—Well, then what country?

—I will keep that a mystery.

—Hopefully not a murder mystery.

—That genre I leave to you, my friend.

—You know, Yuliya, I really like you. You are very quick. I hope you won't warn Saakashvili.

—I thought you complained I was slow.

—Mentally quick.

—So you wanted to flatter me and you still managed an insult.

—You are quick. See?

———————

Three hours later, at Charles de Gaul, Yuliya waved me goodbye. I have no idea what she was thinking. Was she my security agent? But if she was, wouldn't she need to accompany me all the way? Or maybe at the other end, there would be another agent?

The alarm went off as I walked through with Murmansk, and I presented my nuclear isotope lab test papers. Oh, yes, you Americans, said an agent. We are familiar with your tests. You love everything nuclear, even nuclear tests.

CHAPTER EIGHTEEN

Intended to be the last chapter for at least one person

THE PLANE LANDED at the Tbilisi airport at four in the morning, with me in a mental haze of Bourgogne reds and Cognac. I navigated through the crowded marbled airport, and a man, who looked like a joyful Stalin, addressed me in Russian, —Taxi? Better rate than the official one. Twenty-five Lari. Hotel?

I drew a thousand Lari out of the ATM machine and gave him a boutique hotel address, the Old City Hotel, just a hundred paces downhill from the Freedom Square. He introduced himself as Alex, sold me a SIM card for my phone for five Lari, recommended restaurants, wine shops, and gave me his card, in case I wanted a ride anywhere in the country.

The hotel featured a top-floor balcony with a view of the castle to the north and to the south the new cathedral, with gold relaying the sun off it, reminded me of the Khazan cross, except here, the entire dome and the side spire roofs were coated in fresh gold. The hotel was surrounded by a wine store, with afternoon and night wine tastings; a pharmacy; a dental office with smiling teeth sign; a Thai massage parlor; and a Catholic church with collapsed walls. The city was predominantly Orthodox as Stalin had deported many Jews as well as a large Lutheran population into deep Siberia. To clear my head from the French wine, I had a double shot of Turkish coffee at a shop which sold Khachapuri, sourdough cheese bread.

I'd never sought a president to meet with. My emails to PR offices of the Georgian president, interior ministry, and so on went ignored. A day passed in a relatively satisfying manner, with my tasting a variety of Georgian dishes, such as kharcho soup and trout in walnut sauce, and several kinds of Saperavi reds. The city looked sooty and Soviet, and the air seemed to have remained there since the Soviet Union, with car exhaust making me dizzy. I took a cab ride, with Alex, across the river to the presidential palace with a glass dome, and checked out the Trinity Cathedral, a replica of the Serbian Orthodox cathedral in Belgrade, but multiplied by three in terms of size. The dome glared in the sun, pure gold, fresh, and clean, unaffected by weather and history, since it was only two years old. Unlike the bronze dome of the Khazan cathedral, which changed color to green, this one would stay the same color.

I thought of getting in touch with the American ambassador, to tell him about how I was abused in Russia, but since I was out of Russia, why would I still hang around the former Soviet Republics? I would do better to present myself as a wine importer in need of a contact, but why with the president and not a minister? And I emerged out of Russia as a privileged person. Maybe I could consider myself an FSB agent? Maybe I was? I had a direct phone line to Putin. I dialed it but there was no answer. I suppose he expected me to figure out the way to Saakashvili. Maybe he has sent half a dozen people to Georgia, a Russian roulette, hoping that one of us would succeed.

I decided on a relatively lame approach. Columbia was Mikheil's and my alma mater; we were her children, and therefore brothers. That might not be enough, but since Saakashvili was a narcissist like most presidents, I thought an interview for a journal could work. It would be best to do it for *Time* magazine or the *New York Times*, but how could I quickly get an assignment, and who would believe me without some kind of journalist ID or letter? But even *Columbia Spectator* might work. A while back, I had written a couple of pieces on fraternity drinking problems, having done splendid research in the fraternities and the bars between 108th and 116th streets on Broadway and Amsterdam. Saakashvilli used to drink in some of those bars. So, doing an interview—hopefully the last one ever for Saakashvili—would work. Promptly, I shot an email to the editor of *Spectator*, an old nerdy friend from the college days, offering to do an interview with the glorious law school alumnus of Columbia, and I got an immediate enthusiastic response. I asked then for a letter of assignment, and I got one. Not only that, but the editor also arranged for a meeting between the two alumni for the following day.

So now I gave Murmansk milk to drink, with predictable digestive results, and with a bit of washing, and much soap, I rescued the little gold capsule with the precious and pernicious contents. I peeked inside at the polonium dusting. And I fed Murmansk a special meal, lamb shashlik. She purred, much relieved, blinking joyously, unaware that she was a first-rate smuggler of nuclear materials.

Saakashvili's driver picked me up in a black BMW, which brought up immediately an unpleasant remembrance of the things past from Liteny. And the driver (this time not Alex) looked familiar as well—but only looked, I hoped and assumed. There's a certain mustachio Caucasus type of men, several types, which seem to get replicated readily, probably all descendants of the same dictators. If eight percent of the population in Mongolia could be traced to Genghis Khan's gonads, perhaps some genome existed in Georgia as well, with a high incidence—perhaps even Genghis Khan's, as he had invaded this area. Probably not Stalin's, because the Comrade was more interested in murder than sex.

—*Zdrastvuyte*, said I.

—Good day, responded the driver. Where may I take you?

—Your English is excellent, I said. Where have you learned it?

—Thank you. This will be a short ride.

—To the President's Palace? Yes, I know, it's five blocks away, we could have walked.

—No, we are going to his private residence in the mountains.

Soon we were above the city. On top of a hill alongside a canyon, a TV and cell phone tower stood high. The river in the gorge below looked green.

—Why is the river so green? I asked.

—Oh it's all the leaves. We had many storms and . . . you know how that goes.

—Not some chemistry from the Soviet Era?

—No. We are part of the EU. Everything is green here.

—I can see that.

Songbirds created an unrepeatable polyphony in liquid tones which floated on the aromatic breezes of wildflowers, lindens, and acacia, with a low buzz of bees as a basal tone. No wonder this region drew Lermontov, Pushkin, and other frozen Russian esthetes, imaginatively and physically. South of all that Russian misery reposed this vivid paradise.

Past Telavi (sounded like Tel Aviv but only accidently) and a couple of churches and fortresses on riverbanks, we drove into an old estate with an arboretum, bamboo garden, and a water fountain. I gazed to the mountains which were grassy almost all the way up to the snowline, way across a river valley. Green, white, and blue layered the distant landscape wonderfully. It was almost like a view of the Rockies, except not so rocky. On a steep mountainside I could make out moving dots, goats and sheep.

Pretty soon I was shaking hands with the tall, somewhat chubby president, surprised by how swollen his hand was. Maybe Saakashvili had kidney problems? Maybe people have already tried to poison him? This could be a polonium ingestion side effect.

—Let's go to the balcony to enjoy this sensational day, the president said. On the other hand, almost every day here is sensational.

We sat on sheepskin upholstered chairs overlooking a river canyon and one of the peaks above the foothills of Caucasus.

—Oh, my friend, I miss the Upper West Side! But before we go down the nostalgia trail, would you like a glass of Georgian wine? White, red, rose?

—Rose, for Rose Revolution, which you started? Unfortunately, I don't like rose.

—Neither do I.

—I'd like a red wine, of course.

—First, a little test. Close your eyes and we'll give you a glass of wine and you have to guess whether it's red or white. Maybe we'll put a scarf over your eyes so you don't cheat.

—Fine, I said. And thought, OK, if I am drinking blindfolded, I have no idea whether I am drinking some kind of drug. What if they know why I am here and . . .

Anyway, I drank the proffered liquid. It was a bit sweet, strong, and I guessed it was some kind of red wine.

Saakashvili laughed and took off my blindfold. –Almost everybody takes it for a red. This white wine is made by the same methods that the reds are made, with skins staying on during fermentation. See, it's actually orange.

—So, you'll have an Orange Revolution.

—Sure, but not here, in Ukraine. My friends from the law school are inviting me to participate. You know, if the politics don't work out here, I can go to Ukraine and help with the reforms there. I hate corruption, I am like an anti-corruption doctor.

—You should come to America then.

—Have some Saperavi reserve. It's only fifty years old—that's the optimum age. I have a few sealed jugs several hundred years old but from experience, I can tell you that it peaks at the age of fifty, just like we will, no? I also have a jug of wine as old as Christ, two thousand years old and sealed. Would you like to try it?

—No, thank you, that sounds too dangerous. Fifty years old, almost like me, sounds dangerous enough.

—Can you pour us some in a horn? He addressed a butler, a dignified man with a wonderful mustache, wearing moccasins, who handed me a gilded hollow horn of a ram.

Saakashvili talked: —The batch was made in the old style—the grapes were buried underground—skin and all—for four months. You know, that's how the first wine was made, accidently, here, eight thousand years ago. It's older than the Biblical world.

—Maybe the Biblical stories couldn't be concocted without the wine? Only a drunk could come up with some of the Scriptures.

—Let's not become sacrilegious now. But yes, I don't think we'd have our crazy religions without wine.

—Oh, with fine wines, how would it be sacrilege?

—You know where the word wine comes from?

—Yes, of course, from ghvino, old Georgian word for wine.

—And that word is older than all the European languages, isn't that something? And then it became one of the key words in the languages. And you all get this word from us. So my friend, with each sip you are doing time travel, to the origins of civilization and one of the oldest words in your language. How many do you speak?

—Only four. I don't want to compete with you. You are a famous polyglot. How many?

—Nine.

—*Nein!?* Wow, this wine is sensational! Powerful, like Primitivo but more interesting.

—And the cool thing is, the alcohol content is only eleven percent but it tastes like fifteen, like a Napa Zin.

—More subtle, less oaky.

—We don't play those tannin games. If you want something strong, we have stuff better than port. Khardanaki. Here, have a shot.

Saakashvili poured a large glassful of it. I had an Adam's-apple-jolting gulp and then Saakashvili took the same glass and had a gulp with his Adam's apple flying up and clicking back into its proper mid-neck range.

—With friends, I like to drink from the same glass, he said. He raised his eyebrows.

This gave me a chill. Next, when I pour the dust into his wine, he'll want me to drink it too? Does he suspect something?

—Sweet, like sherry, and strong, yes, like port. I practiced my wine enthusiast language, but without over-the-top adjectives.

Pretty soon, after tasting enough history of the world, I was tempted to start the interview. I might ask wrong questions, like, Is it true that you are in the habit of chewing your silk tie? Saakashvili's tie did look a little crumpled at the end. Silk may not be all that unpleasant to the tongue, probably better than tobacco: it's some kind of worm saliva digested with enzymes. Maybe it's beautiful worm shit?

And should I ask Saakashvili about growing up without a father? We had the same sadness in common. Or about fits of rage and reputation for throwing cell phones at cabinet members? And suicidal tendencies of climbing rooftops and leaning over? Maybe these were rumors spread by Russians. That could be a good topic of conversation for an interview, but what if it provoked a temper tantrum?

—Would you like a little sightseeing tour? Saakashvili asked.

—How could I say no to that?

He pointed below: in the bamboo grove among blue peacocks sat a red helicopter.

As we kept tossing glasses back, I worried. Not only was it clear that I was an alcoholic but also that I was not great assassin material. At what moment to slip the dust into one of the ghvino glasses? And after drinking six or seven, will Mikheil—by now we were on first-name terms—drink one more? And now that we were passing the same glass back and forth, like a joint, I might have to drink my own poison. Maybe that was a precaution he used, to first let me drink from the same glass before he does. As a powerful man, he was an aphrodisiac incarnate—-Kissinger's motto, power is an aphrodisiac, which means, someone will get fucked—he must have exchanged bacterial culture with many women (and men by proxy), so drinking a haze of his saliva left on the wineglass rim might be quite risky, medically speaking.

—We can't go back to wine now, you know, Mikheil said. *Wein nach Bier, dass rate ich dir! And Weinbrandt nach Wein . . . Alors,* some cognac.

—I know Zakarpatski, the Ukrainian cognac, but none from the Caucasus. Is there Zakavkaski?

—First, some herb grappa, Cha-cha.

—What will happen to our interview at this rate?

—I am so glad to have a brother from New York visiting. You know, we Georgians think of our guests as sent directly by God. That's a tradition.

—Our alma mater Columbia is a god!

I laughed at that, thinking of Putin. That's some god, sending assassins, but it wouldn't be the first time. There surely is a Biblical story like that.

—Enron, Saakashvili said. —We do research on all our guests, so I know a fair amount about you.

He gave me a gaze, his brown eyes catching sunset rays. His oiled black hair, which probably by now should have some grays, glistened.

What chemistry did he use to keep it black? "Paint It, Black," the Stones' melody, resounded in my head.

What does he know? Does he know all about my Russian adventures, days with Putin, and the poison in my pocket? How would he know? Who would tell him? Yuliya is his spy? His and Putin's? Is she a double or triple spy? Maybe even spying for Hungary. That would be a greater feat than a gold at the Olympics. They could be friends from Saakashvili's days of studying for the first law degree in Kiev.

—Have a shot of Kazbegi! Saakashvili poured a golden-colored liquid, with a bit of rose aroma and honey undertone, sweet and warming. And I didn't say anything. The ensuing silence made me shiver.

Saakashvili smiled. —You worked for Enron and made lots of money.

—Made and lost.

—That's how it goes. And you have friends who work in the wine business, and that may be your next line of work? You know, I might help you there. I am not naïve, and I know that's what you hope to get out of this meeting, but that's cool. Let's organize a wine export-import business. We have distributors for Georgian wines, but they are not good enough. They tend to think of our wines as budget, cheap wines, $8.99 a bottle, you know.

—Now that you've lost the Russian market, which accounted for seventy percent of your exports, there must be a lot of wine waiting to be sold.

—Exactly. Usually when you have an oversupply you lower the price but I want to raise it.

—Avia from Yugoslavia started out as $1.99 a bottle in the States. It's like Kia and Yugo translated to wine. Kia is becoming more and more expensive and Yugo is dead.

—But you can't compare Slovene wines and ours. We can do the high-end wine and brandy exports, fifty dollars a bottle, like Grgich.

—A fantastic idea. Yes, I know Grgich: a clever wine producer and businessman. You know, I was about to propose that to you, the high end, and you beat me to the punch.

—So to speak, he said. Weren't you surprised when you got to the States that people drank punch—all these fruits juices and sugars with booze?

—When I got to the States, I was twelve. No punch yet. Excuse me, I'll have to go to the restroom.

—What kind? I do have a traditional Roman-style vomitorium, too, if that's what's needed. My guests often can't go through the whole round of tasting the history of winemaking and cognac without a visit or two.

—Oh, no, I have a better stomach than that.

—But you should visit the room anyway. It's made out of gilded green marble, just wonderful. When you are there, you feel like an eel.

—Thank you, maybe later. And by the way, the Roman vomitorium didn't mean a place for drunks to vomit, but simply an exit corridor—where the stadium would be emptied of the spectators.

—Thank you for the disappointing tidbit of knowledge. Kind of fascinating that we are so eager to project vomit into the Roman history. Anyway, I don't care whether the Romans had a special room for vomiting. I do.

I went to the bathroom, in which everything was made out of golden-hued marble. I took out the gold capsule. I peeked into it. To pour or not to pour? I could just get rid of it and forget about Putin. I put it back in my pocket. But then I worried that if I had so much radiation right next to my scrotum, I might develop testicular cancer, and it wouldn't be as glorious as the supreme doper, Lance Armstrong's.

Suddenly that thought took hold of me. I had a clear choice—either to pour a dose after tasting another kind of brandy before passing it back to Saakashvili, under the table, while laughing at a joke, or not to. If I did, I could go back to Russia, live in a luminous apartment right on Griboedova, bathed in the light of Franz Marc's paintings, and vacation near Lake Baikal in a Siberian tiger preserve...but I'd still be a Putin's prisoner. Or new plan B, throw the capsule off the terrace into the woods, and go back to the States, import fine wines, vacation in Georgia, and occasionally listen to Saakashvili's jokes, as familiar and as Soviet as they were. Of course, I'd have to worry that I would be assassinated by Putin's agents, and that could decrease the joys. That plan didn't seem as glorious as the first, but it was easier and more humane, more moral. Why did I buy into Putin's plan? Am I drugged and zombified ever since my visit to his palace? I'd never killed anyone, why would I now? Just for a somewhat more luxurious life? Or out of fear that if I don't follow through on this mission, something terrible would happen to me?

—You've probably heard this joke, Saakashvili said, throwing back his red tie behind his neck. —Whenever I drink a lot, I start telling Soviet jokes, you know.

—I have similar tendencies.

—*Tito dies and Lucifer says, Let me show you a few possibilities. In the sixth circle Brezhnev has infinite sex with Marilyn Monroe. Tito says, may I have this kind of punishment? Certainly, Lucifer answers, but let me point out that it's a punishment for Marilyn Monroe, not Brezhnev. They go on to the next circle: Hitler is in hot oil up to his mustache. And next to him stands Stalin, in hot oil to his knees. WTH, says Tito, I thought Stalin killed five times as many people as Hitler. True enough, answers Lucifer, but you should understand that he stands on Lenin's shoulders.*

Here Saakashvili laughed so that his belly shook and his eyes vanished in the folds of his chubby cheeks, and just at that moment,

I was tempted once again to slip the nuclear dusting into brandy, and visualized tossing the capsule over a tall cedar tree, possibly a cedar of Lebanon, at a black raven, who flew off, squawking.

—Even ravens like this joke, said Mikheil, fingering his red tie.

I looked at him blankly. I didn't hate him. Could I kill him to have a luxurious and hedonistic life in Russia—maybe even a soulful one as I would certainly have reasons for penitence?

Mikheil said, —Would you like another Soviet joke? Or a Georgian one? We tell more Armenian jokes than Georgian.

I gulped the wine and was too drunk to remember to answer his questions.

—So you are serious, you'd like to start importing Georgian wines, he said. Into what countries?

—U.S. and Brazil.

—Why Brazil.

—Why no?

—Now, that's a silly pun. But that means the wine is good. Let's go back to Tbilisi and do more wine tasting. I think one evening won't be enough. Tomorrow I am busy receiving Netanyahu, but a day later would be fine.

Two days later, a government driver took me to the castle above Tbilisi. Saakashvili, the Polish ambassador, and I sat on the stone balcony. We drank white wines as the evening was warm, and the problem for me was that I couldn't feel the white wine enough as though I was drinking lemonade. I said to the Polish ambassador, —You must be proud of Chopin and Polonium?

—Yes, Madame Curie, of course, he said. She had no idea that it would be used as poison in assassinations. Putin's favorite choice.

—Don't worry, Saakashvili said, his agents can use cars, grenades, handguns, MiGs, plutonium, polonium, strychnine.

—She died from radiation exposure, the ambassador said. Her bone marrow dried up.

—By the way, I said, Vladimir Arutyunian—did you ever find out who sent him?

—Who are you asking? asked Mikheil. —I have some ideas but no proofs. Anyway, I took it as a compliment. You aren't a real president unless someone tries to assassinate you.

—Were there other attempts on your life?

—Yes, of course. If it becomes too much, I will just move to Ukraine and become a governor. And maybe later, a prime minister.

—What an idea! said the ambassador. What an optimist you are, certainly thinking outside the box. Or outside the borders anyway.

—We have already discussed that possibility—if I get kicked out of Georgia. . .

—How much wine does Poland import from Georgia? I asked the ambassador.

—Not nearly enough. Now that Russia, which accounted for eighty percent of the Georgian wine exports, no longer takes the wine, we have a terrific opportunity.

—Excellent. Maybe we can help, I said.

—You are good, Saakashvili said. You've already started your new job! The way to go. Sky is the limit.

—It is, I said, and pulled out the golden capsule with polonium-210 and threw it down the hill, nearly hitting a crouching black cat, whom I noticed only now.

—What did that cat do to you? asked Saakashvili. And the stone you threw glittered like gold.

—All that glitters is not gold. Oh, by the way, I know a Polish joke, I said.

—Who doesn't? said the Polish ambassador.

—OK, I said. *Putin lands in Warsaw and goes through the customs. Name? Vladimir Vladimirovich Putin. Occupation? Not yet.*

When I realized I was the only one laughing, I wanted to find the restroom. They probably knew the joke and maybe had reasons not to like it. It was raining, warm rain. Wobbly, I walked to the staircase and while gazing at the river and the illuminated bridge and various places of worship, I lost balance and flew down the stairway, at least twenty tall granite stairs. I hit the iron parapet with my left side. The iron knocked the air out of me. A jolt of air in my trachea and my ribs being smashed hurt simultaneously. Is this the end? For a moment I wanted to do nothing but lie unconscious in the pissy rain. Saakashvili and the ambassador were holding me up, and discussing, Do you think he broke his spine? Or only the ribs? Is he alive? I don't remember much after that. I slept, dreaming that I was in Tehran, being beaten with lead-filled Billy clubs, accused of spying on their nuclear program for Israel.

I woke up on a wide bed. If I moved a little, the lower left hurt excruciatingly. I thought, Oh, good news, that was only a nightmare. I am not in Tehran. I am in Tbilisi. Bad news, I am in Tbilisi: my ribs must be broken, most of the left rack of them, as I can't move without a sensation that a knife was lodged inside.

Despite the pain, I felt tickling on my side. Murmansk was licking my lower thorax. Who undressed me and put me here? And where is here?

I looked around—red velvet drapes and below, a cat litter box and a bowl of milk. Europeans believe milk is cat food. How often in nature do you see an adult cat sucking on teats of let's say a goat? On the other hand, how often do you see in the wild an adult cat eating unnatural industrial food? Will a nurse show up? Don't I need help?

Murmansk kept licking raspily. There was no bruise, no sign of injury on my thorax. How is that possible? No external but plenty of internal damage? Am I just imagining that I need imaging? I moved a bit, and the stabbing pain recurred.

I turned on my laptop, which was opened on the bed next to me. I sat up with enormous effort, gasping, and then googled. Strangely enough, I didn't like extreme pain. With rib fractures there's a sixteen percent likelihood of death. That's counting all sorts of accidents where there's other damage too. Well, maybe this fall of mine falls under other damage, because how would I know that my spine actually was not broken? That a rib was not cutting my lungs, spleen, and kidneys?

I looked through my jean's pockets. The capsule with the polonium was gone. Maybe I should have poured the polonium into Saakahsvili's glass after all. Maybe Saakashvili's death would have appeased Putin and led to world peace, with Georgia not joining NATO? But even if I had tried to poison the President, he probably would have not been affected right away, and this whole sequence of events with my falling would have been the same. Now, how about if when I was already blitzed on white wines—I will never import whites—they took out the poison from my pocket and poured it into my wine? Maybe whoever took me to the hotel found the golden capsule and stole it. Maybe they just wanted the gold but if they opened the capsule, good luck to them. Just inhaling the dust would give them lung cancer. And only then did I remember that I had tossed away the capsule, enthusiastic about Saakashvili and my future in wine.

I imagined I had a one in six chance to be killed by my ribs perforating vital organs, and one in six that I was poisoned by plutonium from peeking into the capsule too often. One in six, like the Russian roulette. Two Russian roulettes would make it approximately one in three—that probable that I will kick the bucket? And add to that the horrific foods I've had for a while, all the cholesterol, liver damage, radiation, my survival is reduced to a fifty percent probability. But this didn't depress me. It almost put me in a good mood. That didn't make sense—I guess I didn't understand myself.

I don't know myself. Socrates didn't know himself, so why should I? Know thyself, he said. And it's true, it's about time I quit drinking wine. None of this would have happened if it hadn't been for red wine. And white wine. Except I might have become a murderer.

EPILOGUE

Bel Horizonte

NEARLY TWO YEARS LATER, in 2008, established as a wine importer specializing in Georgian and Slovenian wines, I took a month off from my work and wrote a novel resembling the preceding pages but with the variant A ending, of poisoning Saakashvili and living in Russia with a Ukrainian gymnast, who was expecting a baby, but X-rays revealed she was carrying a crossover between human and Amur tiger, too large to go through the birth channel and therefore a dictator Caesarian section was required—a fantasy, some kind of failed *Master and Margarita*.

After finishing the draft of the novel, I sent it out to various publishers in the States, who all turned it down, but a publisher in Spain accepted it, saying it was a novel in the Spanish picaro tradition, and immediately had it translated into Catalan and Spanish and printed. El Publisher, Pedro Pujol (pseudonym, of course), said that since Russia had just started bombing Gori—Stalin's birthtown—in Georgia, it was the right moment to publish a novel about current affairs in Russia. Seize the day, he said. I protested that there was no rush. Russia would always be in the news. When wasn't Russia in the news? If we missed this war, well, there would be another one. (Plus, it crossed my mind that if I published the novel, I couldn't travel to

Russia again, and I wanted to. I still daydreamed of finding Yuliya.) Don Pedro invited me to tour in Spain. I still couldn't sleep on my left side, and in the morning, I'd have pains in the ribs or below them. Maybe I have recovered and have neuralgia. Anyhow, *l'chaim!* Life is great.

For some reason, I had never made it to Spain before. Years before, I had met a Croatian exile, who had—once he'd escaped from Tito's camps—worked as Franco's gynecologist, supervising the elite bordellos in Madrid. I related this to my editor, Pedro, who said, This would make a fine title for a novel, *Franco's Gynecologist.* Impeccably dressed in a blue shirt and fine crimson leather shoes, Pedro smoked unfiltered Chesterton's, drank gin, and had a mischievous glint in his eyes, enjoying anything absurd and strange. No wonder he likes my work, I thought as I looked at my Spanish literary patron saint. It's a bad sign for anybody to like my work, so I had reason to worry about him. I was trying to quit drinking, to devote my brain and liver to sobriety and writing, but in Spain I would still make an exception, with the classic prayer from St. Augustine: *God, make me chaste, but not yet.* Maybe one could adapt the prayer to different regions, *God, make me chaste in America, but not in Spain, please!*

Don Pedro, Murmansk, and I arrived in Valencia in the early evening on a fast train from Barcelona, with the sky still blue and the lights of the city bouncing off the buildings. We took a cab to our hotel, with Murmansk meowing in her luxurious pet carrier. It was a bit embarrassing that I traveled like a cat lady. She never quite got used to travel but she could take it. Valencia is sensationally bright, with most buildings in the center made of white stone and the streets paved with slabs of polished marble. Right next to the train station stands a red brick bullfighting arena. Beyond the palm trees, I had an illusion that I was seeing Algiers.

In the streets there were all sorts of accents, different from Spanish, maybe Catalan, but then I realized, even Russian. One remark-
able thing about Valencia and Spain in general was the absence of
children in the streets, and the average age looked to be old.

The streets next to our hotel Astoria were angled, cobbled, beautiful. A nightclub, Bel Horizonte, blinked its neon blue against the
white walls.

—Should we check it out? Don Pedro said.

We walked down the stairs. At the entrance stood a man in
sneakers who looked like a soccer player, with thick thighs and no
belly protruding. —Come in, no cover charge.

From the darkness of the downstairs club wafted a strong smell
of a variety of perfumes and soaps. We descended the marble staircase. On our right appeared an empty red-velvet room.

—That is the first circle of hell, said Pedro. Abandon all hope
you who enter!

Inside, there were a dozen women, and one man in a black suit.
The floor was black, the walls were black, and the bar was lined with
mirrors and bottles of Scotch.

—What would you like? Pedro asked. It's on me.

—Something basic, like Black Label on the rocks.

Pedro got gin and tonic.

—You know, I commented, it's disappointing that a Spaniard
would drink something like that—that's a drink made for those who
don't produce good wine or whiskey.

—Oh, wine makes me tense. Scotch may have too much flavor,
but of course, you should try the Spanish brandy.

A pale black-haired woman in high heels came over to me and
said, —You are looking at me? Why? You want me to dance?

She jumped up on a little circular stage with a pole and didn't
undress. Her face: somewhat slanted eyes, high cheekbones, a narrow

nose, slightly aquiline, and a well-defined narrow chin, with full lips. Her legs and her thighs were unusually lean.

—You should dance with her, Don Pedro said.

—Probably you should if you like her.

—No, I am a rookie at this. I'll see how it works.

I had only a few thick one-euro coins. I put two coins on the edge of the dance floor, and the women, when they saw what I did, giggled. A positive wave of merriment moved through the basement.

—What is your name? the dancer asked, and I said, David.

—Marina. She put her nails in the back of my shirt and tickled me. From her sweat, from her dancing, I could smell her.

—You give out your real name? Pedro said.

—If people usually give wrong names, she will not believe David is my name.

Marina walked away and drank Sprite.

—Where do you think she is from? Don Pedro asked.

—He ordered another round, and he smoked while a stately woman in jeans talked to him. That same woman had taken the coins from the dance floor. I was startled because she resembled Masha from Russia (Ukraine), although plumper, maybe carrying fifteen pounds more. Many Russians, once they move abroad, eat better and don't walk so much, and consequently put on weight. She was not looking in my direction. It could very well be her, I thought, and maybe she was tracking me. She had been so close to the police, why hadn't it crossed my mind that she was one of them? The FSB agents, if they were to track me, would know my novel had come out in Spain—they saw the announcements in the papers. (Moreover, they had probably hacked my computer and have already read it. They could have at least corrected my Russian!) But do agents, other than the literary ones, read novels anymore?

—You seem absentminded, Don Pedro said. —This is not a place to be absentminded.

—Don Pedro, you go ahead, dance. I am not in the mood. Do you think anyone will read my novel?

—Don't worry about that, it will be a hit.

—I am worried even about that. If it's a hit, Russian agents will be after me. Either way it's bad. You know Putin's agents killed that journalist Anya Politkovskaya.

—Yes, but she had a lot of hard-core information.

—And I don't?

Don Pedro took a sip of gin and smiled.

Marina sat on the dance floor, leaning her head sideways; she waited, languished, in some kind of anguish, looking like a wounded black swan, shining and shimmering in the light. She lifted her gaze pessimistically, with a certain Balkan or trans-Caucasian gloom.

In the meanwhile, five young men descended. They all looked trim and fit, like UFC fighters. One of them had a broken nose, and he reminded me of my driver on Liteny, and one of them was tall, but it would be hard to find distinguishing features in the others. I looked at the boxer's nose again and wondered, What's the likelihood that it's the cop who did the hit and run?

—I don't like these guys, I said.

—Russian mafia, that's my guess.

—Their servants. Do you think Marina is a sex slave? Should we take her out of here, save her?

—Kidnap her?

—Why not. Or report to the police.

—Don't be naïve.

We walked out of the club and had one more round of drinks in the square in front of the hotel at an outdoor café. A man with curly black hair and strong eyebrows played the violin, the Hungarian char-dash with southern Balkan strains as though rearranged by Bregovic.

—You don't seem to be enjoying the music, Don Pedro said. Don't worry, your novel will be a success. There are reviews coming out in the major dailies, nearly all of them.

—Maybe he's classically trained?

—Strange that there are no men going to the club, said Pedro.

—Maybe because it's Monday. Maybe that's a bad day for business. Barbers don't work on Mondays, perhaps gentlemen don't visit such clubs Mondays either. Maybe gentlemen never do.

At the Hotel Astoria, I withdrew three hundred euros from an ATM, and when I turned around, I saw Marina drinking soda—or gin and tonic?—leaning against the polished oak bar.

—Hola, Marina!

—My name is Angelina.

—But what is your real name?

—Angelina for real. The other is my underground name.

—You are from Moldova?

—Yes, from Russia.

—The country you come from should stay the same, not change every two hours like your name.

—Maybe every five years. The countries I come from change borders all the time.

She wore jeans and a blue sweater as though it was a cold day, but maybe for southerners it would be.

—How often do you go home?

—What is home?

—What town? Bucharest?

—Not in a long time. And it's not Bucharest.

—What's the name of your hometown?

—I won't tell you. You don't need to know.

When we passed by the front desk, the clerk gave us a long look. In the elevator, she kissed me. Her lips were creamy with red lipstick, and beyond it, it was salty, as though she had eaten anchovies.

When we got into the room, she went to the bathroom to shower. She was taking her time. And of course, I had enough time to think. I would give her all the cash I had but would not have sex with her. I could rant and rave in the Dostoevsky Underground man tradition, baring my soul and self-contempt but how would that help her or me? I was tempted to feel noble for not indulging in the carnal business and for supporting Liza or Marina or whoever she was but the fact is I had a bad intuition about my situation.

I looked out the window. The five men circled around their white BMW which was cranking and spitting out blue smoke. Masha or her double stood on the side and gestured for them to turn off the car. The Liteny cop or his double opened the trunk.

I called up Pedro, and said, —Look, can you get us a car, rent a car? We got to get the hell out of here.

—Why? Is the Russian mafia after you once again? I got your number, you are paranoid. I thought that was just an artistic imagination for your novel. I am sure Putin could care less about absurd little novels published in Spain.

—You think it's just a little novel? You didn't talk like that before.

—You have ten interviews lined up for this morning. Why are you sabotaging your career? She's with you?

—How did you know?

—I was in the back of the lobby. Does she have papers on her?

—I don't know.

—Without papers, it's not going to be easy.

—She is taking a shower. She seems to like it, already twenty minutes.

—Where is her purse? Quickly check her ID.

—Why would I? It could be a fake. Just rent a car. Nobody accompanied her.

—OK, I'll wait for you at the back entrance in fifteen minutes.

The shower was still on, and the room had become steamy.

We drove through the narrow streets in a circle, and then passed the bullfighting Coliseum-like stadium. I looked around, to see whether any cars would follow us. My heart thumped out of rhythm. What if Marina had swallowed some poison and passed out in the shower? Maybe she's eaten polonium? Everything is possible and hardly anything probable.

Pedro said, —We must stop somewhere for a gin and tonic.

—You want a DUI? We'll drink in Barcelona. Do you think we should have brought her along? Maybe you need an au pair?

—But I don't need an agent. Paranoia is a contagious disease.

—Can we publish my novel under a pseudonym?

—You were desperate to be famous, and now you already want anonymity.

He sped up. Murmansk meowed and, when that didn't help, farted. I turned around, expecting to see the white BMW and blue smoke. If the Russians haven't bothered me about Saakashvili earlier, why would they be after me now? Don't they have better things to do? I laughed, How could I be so silly? It's all great. The sun was rising and seagulls diving into the white-capped sea.

I leaned out the window to feel the cool dawn air, and as I inhaled the aroma of pine needles and sea waters, in the rear-view I caught sight of a vermillion print on my left cheek, resembling the lip print on the dead man on Griboedova.

ACKNOWLEDGMENTS

I AM THANKING several people who have helped me with the novel:

Michael A. Saltman for the fellowship at the Black Mountain Institute in Las Vegas to spend several months of uninterrupted work and for interrupting the work occasionally for our thrilling ping-pong matches.

Michelle Dotter and Steven Gillis, for publishing this work, and Michelle Dotter also for guiding me through the revision.

Steven Dunn for residencies at the Eastern Frontier Artist Retreat on Norton Island in Maine and for his hearty laughter which encouraged me in writing some of the silly scenes.

Several people have given me excellent feedback: Buzz Poole, John Goldbach, Irina Iavorskaia, Mariya Gusev, Kodi Scheer, and Jack Schiff.

And thank you, David Stromberg, for giving me the assignment to write a story for the St. Petersburg Noir anthology. Never mind that the anthology did not come out but died mysteriously in a noir fashion. Out of the story evolved the novel. And thank you Mikhail Iossel and Jeff Parker for inviting me to Russia several times and for introducing me to the charismatic place.

I am also thanking the Fulbright Commission for granting me a Senior Research Fellowship at St. Petersburg State University in Russia, and Yaddo and Canada Council for the Arts for time and space to write. Thank you Patricia Caswell (for residencies at the Hermitage Artist Retreat) and Milena Deleva and Yana Genova for the residency at the Next Page Foundation in Sofia, Bulgaria. Elizabeth Kostova and Milena for hospitality at the Sozopol Fiction festivals.

Excerpts of the novel have appeared in much different forms in the *Barcelona Review, KGB Lit Review, Narrative Magazine*, the *Southern Review*, and the *Fence Magazine*, and I am grateful to the editors of the journals.

ABOUT THE AUTHOR

JOSIP NOVAKOVICH is a Croatian-American writer who resides in Canada. His work has been translated into Croatian, Bulgarian, Indonesian, Russian, Japanese, Italian, and French, among other languages. He was a finalist for the Man Booker International Prize in 2013 and also received the American Book Award from the Before Columbus Foundation, the Whiting Writer's Award, and a John Simon Guggenheim Memorial Foundation Fellowship for Fiction, as well as a fellowship from the National Endowment for the Arts. His work has appeared in *The Paris Review, Threepenny, Ploughshares*, and many other journals, and has been anthologized in *Best American Poetry, The Pushcart Prize*, and *O. Henry Prize Stories*. He teaches English at Concordia University in Montreal, Canada.